Mercedes

The Shackleford Legacies Book Two

Beverley Watts

BaR Publishing

Contents

Chapter One

Nathaniel Harding reluctantly opened his eyes, wincing at the brightness piercing his eyeballs. He might have had one too many brandies the night before, but he couldn't let the anniversary of dear daddy's death go unmarked. As the window finally swam into focus, he noticed that the bottom half was entirely blocked with ... bloody hell, was that snow? Swearing, he rolled out of bed and hurried to the window, only to stare in disbelief at the sea of white. It was *April* for God's sake.

He rubbed a hand over the stubble covering his chin as his befogged brain tried to make sense of the completely foreign landscape. Abruptly, he remembered that his monthly supplies were due today and if he wasn't to starve, he needed to clear a path to his front door, and quickly.

With another, more colourful expletive, he hurriedly began pulling on his clothes. His dog, Ruby, stared at him in disbelief through one bleary eye, before burrowing back into the crumpled bedclothes. Nate shook his head, knowing she'd be out of bed the minute he walked through the door.
As he approached the top of the stairs, he paused for a second, staring down into the gloom below him, absently noting the missing banister spindles, the rotten planks making the stairs a death trap for the unwary. Downstairs in the large reception hall, the panelling was riddled with woodworm – the pieces that were left that is. The rest had long since gone for firewood.

The drawing room, the library, the dining room ... simply more of the same. And the kitchen – if it could be called such? Any minute now, he fully expected the whole lot to come crashing down around his ears.

Carlingford Hall. His inheritance. His father's last joke.

Nate's scrutiny of his questionable kingdom was interrupted by the predicted clicking of claws on the wooden floor. He turned his head to watch Ruby stretch, her bottom high in the air. A quick shake and a desultory wag of her tail followed.

'I'm not keen either, Roo,' Nate muttered, starting down the stairs.

Minutes later, he was shrugging on his old great coat and forcing his way out into the snow, already nearly a foot deep in places. Looking up, he swore again. The flakes were thick, falling from a sky the colour of whalebone. There was no way a horse and cart would get through to the house, and if the snow continued falling like this, digging would be worse than useless.

Nate blew into his hands, trying to decide what to do. His supplies were coming from Corsham, but he had no way of knowing whether the driver would even attempt to get through. Likely the main road would still be passable with the number of carriages using it, but beyond that...?

He shook his head and looked down at Ruby shivering beside him. There was really no choice. He'd have to saddle Duchess and go into town himself. At least he'd be able to bring back enough to feed the three of them until the weather improved.

And with the cold as biting as it was, he'd have the perfect excuse to cover his face.

***

Mercedes Stanhope tucked her hands under her armpits in a

vain effort to keep them warm. It was ironic that the weather in the Cotswolds was significantly colder than it had been in Loch Lomond. Indeed, the sun had shone almost continuously throughout her month's stay at Caerlaverock with Jenny and Brendon - though her best friend's husband of ten months had repeatedly assured her that such clement weather was not typical of the Highlands of Scotland.

She'd started the long journey back to the New Forest five days ago, and the weather had steadily worsened until finally the squalling rain turned to heavy snow. She could only hope the main road remained passable until they reached their final overnight stop before Cottesmore.

She glanced over at her two companions, snoring loudly in opposite corners of the carriage and shook her head, stifling a weary grin.

When she'd first accepted her best friend's invitation to Scotland, Mercedes realised she'd need at least one chaperone to make the long journey with her. However, she hadn't considered that the role might be filled by her step-grandparents. Especially as Reverend Shackleford had been returned from Scotland less than six months.

Apparently, according to Jennifer's brother Peter, the clergyman had inexplicably made a friend in Brendon Galbraith's father, Dougal – though Peter assured her that if either were questioned about their friendship, they would deny it strenuously, likely including a few colourful insults in their repudiation.

The Reverend had therefore magnanimously offered to accompany Mercy on her visit, insisting that his wife Agnes came along on this occasion, presumably to support his chaperoning activities - though where he'd got the idea that Agnes was a champion of a young woman's finer sensibilities, she had no idea. Indeed, as far as Mercedes was aware, neither of her step-grandparents would recognise a finer sensibility if it wacked them on the head.

In actual fact, Augustus and Agnes Shackleford were very much the last two people her father, the Earl of Cottesmore trusted to take care of his eldest daughter's morals - or anything else for that matter. It was an opinion he did very little to hide.

Unfortunately, the eldest daughter in question was in truth possessed of very few *finer sensibilities*. She was however possessed of a mostly well-hidden stubborn streak and had made no bones about the fact that she would marry the first man to cross her path if her father did not allow the visit.

While most fathers might well have been happy to hear such an avowal since Mercy was about to enter into her third season, the fact that she'd come under the dubious influence of her Shackleford relatives at the tender age of eight, put the fear of God into the Earl's heart.

So, with great reluctance, he threw in the towel and allowed Mercy to visit Jennifer in Scotland.

Along with Reverend and Agnes Shackleford.

The month at Caerlaverock with her closest friend - who also happened to be her cousin by marriage - had been glorious. Her step-grandmother's supposed supervisory role had entirely taken place from a newly acquired chaise longue in the small sitting room, while the Reverend had spent the whole time spreading God's word to workers in the local whisky distilleries, leaving Mercy to spend her time assisting Jennifer and Brendon with the building of Caerlaverock's new school for orphans. In between, she roamed the hills and valleys around Loch Lomond with only the Reverend's little dog, Flossy, and Fergus, Brendon's wolfhound for company.

She'd been able to push her upcoming third season to the farthest recesses of her mind - until the very moment she left

Caerlaverock five days ago. And as the days passed, her anxiety had only increased. She would be home at Cottesmore for barely a week before travelling to London with her father and stepmother and three half siblings.

And this time she had to make a good match. No more declaring a bored indifference with the marriage mart and fobbing off potential suitors whilst secretly waiting for a man who would sweep her off her feet.

She wasn't afraid that her father would force her into a match she didn't want. But neither could she remain at Cottesmore for the rest of her life. Not that her stepmother, Chastity, would ever wish her gone. Mercy knew her adopted mother loved her dearly.

In truth, she wanted to be the chatelaine of her own home, but despite her pragmatic declarations to the contrary, she wanted it with a man who loved her by her side.

Mercedes sighed and turned her attention to the seemingly endless fall of snow visible through the window. As she stared out into the increasingly colourless landscape, she felt a sudden moment of disquiet. Biting her lip, she hugged Flossy to her, taking comfort in the little dog's warm body snuggled inside her cloak. As far as she was aware, there was only the Black Swan Inn between here and Corsham. The carriage was travelling apace, but not alarmingly so. She could only assume that Arthur, the lead coach driver was confident they would reach their destination without too much trouble. If she remembered correctly, the inn was on this side of the town.

***

'You're certain her carriage will be stopping here?'

'The coach driver told Smiffy that Stanhope 'ad already paid fer the rooms. Private parlour an' everythin'.'

'Who is she travelling with?'

5

'Coach driver got a bit suspicious o' 'is questions and Smiffy din't want to push it, but she ain't goin' ter be on 'er own. Chits like 'er don't go anywhere wi'out a bloody nursemaid.'

'What time did they leave Tewkesbury?'

'Jus' after eleven milord. There ain't no other inn between there an' 'ere. An' with the weather closin' in, they'll not be tempted to try and get past Corsham to Salisbury. I reckon they should be arrivin' jus' as it starts to get dark. Perfect timing.'

The man shook his head. 'I won't take her today. We'll only have one chance to grab her. Tonight, we find out who she's travelling with. Let the bitch have her last supper.' He patted his coat pocket. 'I already have the licence, and once I have her, all I have to do is get her to the priest.'

***

'When the deuce did it start snowing?' The Reverend cast an incredulous look through the carriage window.

'Not long after we left Tewkesbury,' Mercy answered with a sigh. 'Initially, I didn't think it would settle, but it doesn't seem to be abating at all.'

'Lawks, snow in April, Augustus! Surely it means we're coming to the end times,' Agnes cried, clutching at the Reverend's arm. 'Promise me you've had a word with the Almighty and apologised for all the misery you've caused me?'

She retrieved a kerchief from her reticule and dabbed it under her eyes, adding. 'I know you've not been much of a husband – lord knows you're too ripe and ready by half - and I can't deny you're a bit of a toad eater. You're nearly always in a devil's own scrape ... and you're deuced good at upsetting people, *and* making a cake of yourself...' she paused and blew her nose before finishing, 'but there's no getting away from the fact that you're the only one I've got.'

The Reverend and Mercy stared at Agnes silently, both lost for words as they digested the matron's catalogue of reproaches. When Mercedes finally glanced over at the Reverend, she couldn't help wincing at the interesting colour of his face. 'I really don't think the snow is apocalyptic, Grandmama,' she inserted hurriedly. 'There truly is no need to worry. I'm sure it will be entirely gone before we recommence our journey tomorrow.'

'Well, I can't deny I'm looking forward to reaching Cottesmore,' Agnes sniffed. 'A nice clean bed without any deuced bedbugs.' She gave her posterior a quick scratch for emphasis.

'I'm sure Mama will be delighted to see both of you,' Mercedes soothed.

Her step-grandfather snorted in answer. 'I'll wager Chastity would rather have her fingernails removed with a rusty spoon.' He waved towards the window and chuckled. 'She might have to put up with us for a bit longer than she'd hoped though if this keeps up.'

'Oh, I'm certain it will be gone in no time,' Mercedes repeated, crossing her fingers under her cloak. 'It is April after all.'

'Snow in April,' Agnes muttered. 'You mark my words; it'll be fire and brimstone next.'

The Reverend raised his eyebrows. 'Well, if it is, I'm sure you've got a potion for it somewhere in your bag.'

**

Hoisting the panniers over Duchess's back, and mounting up behind them, Nate whistled to Ruby who was busy nosing at something particularly noxious mixed in with all the snow in the gutter. He'd managed to purchase enough provisions to last him a sennight though he doubted the unseasonal spell of weather would last that long.

Nudging the mare with his feet, he walked her carefully along Corsham high street, taking care to avoid the deeper drifts of snow gathering at the side of the road. Not that the centre of the street was much better, covered with a crisscross of muddy white slush, effectively concealing any hidden stones and rocks.

Despite his cautiousness, as he broke free of the last houses on the edge of the town, the horse began limping. Swearing under his breath, Nate stopped the mare and dismounted, patting Duchess's flank as he lifted the affected hoof. As he raised her leg, she favoured him with a quick irritable nip on his shoulders. Accustomed to her bad temper, he tapped her nose before crouching down to inspect the hoof. Almost immediately he spotted a stone embedded in her shoe, its sharp edge slicing into the tender flesh underneath.

'Fiend seize it,' he muttered to himself, letting her foot go and rising back to his feet. The stone needed removing, but to do so before getting her inside might make things worse rather than better. The stone would almost certainly cause a bruise which in turn could turn to an abscess, and walking her on the hard, snow-covered ground for another three miles... He grimaced, dragging off the scarf covering his lower face in frustration. She needed to be stabled overnight, and since he'd be unable to continue on foot carrying his supplies, he'd have to stay with her.

Running his hand through his unkempt shoulder length hair, Nate squinted through the still heavily falling snow. The carriage tracks outlining the road were already being covered by fresh snow. There really was no time to lose. He shook his head, staring up at the heavens. Bloody snow – in April.

If he remembered correctly, there was an inn a little further along the main road. He couldn't remember exactly how far since he didn't usually pass it, preferring to take a short cut from Carlingford whenever he was forced into Corsham - one that avoided the usually busy main road as much as possible. Today however, the road was deserted, since clearly he was the only person bacon-brained enough to venture out in such filthy weather. Taking hold of Duchess's bridle, he urged the mare onwards, walking beside her to reduce the weight on her back. Ruby trotted happily along, darting in and out of the snow drifts collecting on the side of the road.

Mentally counting how much coin he dared spend, Nate decided he'd simply request a couple of blankets and sleep in the stables with Duchess - providing there was enough room of course.

And at least the equine guests wouldn't be spending the evening staring at his face.

Chapter Two

Percy Noon shivered and frowned up at the unseasonal weather. While there was only the lightest smattering of snow in South Devon, he suspected the story was very different further up the country. Indeed, not half an hour earlier, he'd overheard Peter Sinclair, Viscount Holsworthy and heir to the Blackmore dukedom, claim that parts of Gloucestershire were underneath over a foot of snow.

Having finished his duties in the church, Percy had stopped off at the Red Lion for a swift tankard of ale before dinner. The Viscount had apparently thought to do the same, having just returned from a sennight's visit with his uncle in Bovey. When Percy walked in, his lordship had been busy entertaining the locals with humorous anecdotes about Anthony Shackleford's first experience of fatherhood - his wife Georgiana had recently delivered of a healthy baby boy they'd named Henry.

'Have you heard from your grandfather, my lord?' Percy asked him.

'Only that they left Caerlaverock five days ago and are expected at Cottesmore any day now.' The Viscount shook his head and took a sip of his ale. 'Though if they're caught up in this filthy weather, they might well be stranded for days. Anthony had a new bed brought down from Exeter and the carpenter told us that all supplies coming from Bath had been held up due to the heavy snow. Over a foot in places the fellow claimed.'

Percy grimaced. 'I do hope the coach driver doesn't think to do anything rash. Much better if they are held up in an inn somewhere until the weather allows safe passage. I can't imagine the snow will continue for very long.'

'Likely you're right, Percy. I hope so anyway for Mercy's sake. Being snowbound with our grandparents for any length of time is not an experience I'd wish on anybody.' He chuckled and patted Percy on the back. 'How's Finn? Still running Lizzy ragged?'

The curate grinned. 'That he is, my lord. And talk – I vow the lad only stops to draw breath.'

Finn was one of the Scottish orphans rescued from slavery nearly a year earlier. On returning to Blackmore from Caerlaverock, the Reverend had unexpectedly brought the lad back with him.

Though Augustus Shackleford had staunchly denied having even the slightest inkling that Percy and Lizzy might consider adopting the foundling, Percy believed otherwise, and the curate would be forever in the Reverend's debt.

The truth was that Finn had made him and Lizzy complete. Though Lizzy had never said anything, Percy couldn't help but notice the shadow of sadness behind her eyes whenever she watched children playing. But since Finn's arrival, his wife had been a different woman. The lad was as bright as a button and twice as quick. He wanted to know everything about everything, and since starting the small school in Blackmore village, he'd come on in leaps and bounds. Though Percy was not sure exactly how old he was, he guessed the boy was around seven.

Though Finn loved to talk, the only slight problem was actually understanding exactly what he was talking *about*, since he still spoke in a very broad Scottish accent and the lad seemed to delight in confusing his adopted parents, causing all three of them much hilarity.

In truth, Percy had never been so happy. He was responsible for the day to day running of the parish of Blackmore and Reverend Shackleford appeared as though he was finally enjoying his newfound freedom – even taking Agnes to Scotland as soon as the opportunity arose – though, in fairness, the only way he'd managed to persuade his wife to abandon her beloved chaise longue in the vicarage parlour, was to ensure a replacement was ready and waiting for her in Caerlaverock.

Of course, Percy hadn't entirely abandoned his concerns for his superior – after all, old habits die hard, and the curate had to admit to missing the Reverend when he was absent – especially their usually impromptu visits to the Red Lion, and if he was being entirely honest, the old rascal's proclivity for nosing into things that were really none of his concern...

Percy sighed and finished his ale, then nodding farewell to the Viscount and his circle of enthralled listeners, he made his way to the door. Once outside, he looked up at the ominous sky and frowned.

In actual fact, he was concerned that the Reverend was somehow in trouble – which was patently ridiculous – but Percy couldn't shake the feeling off, nonetheless.

In truth, this wasn't the first time he'd had such a feeling – indeed he'd experienced it on numerous occasions. And every time, the foreboding had preceded a turn of events that convinced him the Almighty was simply warning him that things were about to go to hell in a handcart...

***

Mercedes sighed with relief when the Black Swan Inn finally appeared round a bend in the road. Agnes had succumbed to her salts nearly two miles back, and by the look on the Reverend's face, only the fact that he was a man of the cloth (and possibly the presence of a witness – two if she counted Flossy) had kept him from actually shoving his beloved out of the carriage.

As their carriage turned off the road, Mercedes caught sight of a lone man walking alongside a horse, head down against the driving snow. Just before he disappeared from view, she spotted a small russet coloured terrier, dancing beside him. She wondered where he was going and why he wasn't riding the horse, then as their carriage clattered into the inn's courtyard, she put him out of her mind.

Half an hour later, she was established in a small but clean bedchamber with a welcome fire roaring in the hearth. Shivering, she pulled off her gloves and unpinned her bonnet, then held out her hands towards the flames to warm them. She thought back to her time in Scotland. It had been wonderful, and a huge part of her wished she could have stayed there, hidden away forever. But life didn't work like that. With a sigh, she turned from the fire, and went to look out of the window. Thankfully, the snow appeared to have stopped.

Leaning her head against the pane, Mercy stared down at the large courtyard. The entrance to the stables was just visible if she cocked her head so. The cobbled area was bustling with several ostlers coming in and out of the stalls, and she hoped that meant the horses were being well cared for. As she watched, a man stepped out wearing a hat pulled low over his face. Moments later he was joined by a small dog. After a few seconds, she realised it was the same man she'd spied walking along the road earlier.

Curiously, she stared down at him. The hat was entirely shielding his face, and for some reason she found herself craning her neck, trying to catch a glimpse of his shadowed features. She watched as he bent down to fuss the small terrier. Clearly the animal was well cared for. But more than that – she could tell the dog was loved.

At length, he stood back up and stretched out his neck, lifting his hand to rub one shoulder in a patently weary gesture. She could finally see that he wore a scarf wrapped around his face and neck. Even from this distance she could tell that his great coat was worn and shabby. His hair was long and tied carelessly back with ... something. More than anything, the man looked like a vagrant. But clearly, he'd had enough coin to stable his horse.

She watched, intrigued as he looked round the courtyard. Most of the ostlers had disappeared. After a few seconds, he lifted his hands and untied the scarf, pushing its folds down onto the top of his shoulders. She gave a stifled gasp and took a half step back. There was no way he could have heard her, but nevertheless, he immediately looked up, and as he did so, the iron-grey clouds suddenly parted to uncover a watery sun, which in turn shone directly onto the man's face, fully revealing the hideous scar that stretched all the way from his left temple down to his chin.

Somehow rooted to the spot, Mercy watched as his eyes found hers, even through the thick mullioned glass. For a second, their gazes held, then his face twisted in a wry smile as he deliberately lifted the scarf and wound it back round his face. Then, with the barest nod, he turned and went back into the stable.

***

Reverend Shackleford uttered a heartfelt sigh of relief as he stepped into the bedchamber. During the last leg from Tewkesbury, he'd felt as though his arse was in grave danger of turning into a pancake. And waking up to the sight of snow – well, if it hadn't been so deuced cold, he might have come out in a cold sweat. Being stranded with Agnes anywhere would provide a challenge for even the bravest soul – but being snowed in with her in the middle of nowhere...

He shuddered and stood in front of the fire, turning his back to warm his tender nether regions. From this angle, the bed looked almost too inviting. Certainly, Flossy thought so since she was already stretched out and snoring. Mayhap he would forgo dinner in favour of an early night. But then, what if they had steak and kidney pudding on the menu? He looked over at the bell pull. A large brandy brought up to the bedchamber while he thought about it seemed an obvious answer.

He sighed in contentment. Fortunately, having so many titled sons-in-law had its advantages since one or the other of them usually stumped up the coin for any overnight stays – including the luxury of separate bedchambers - though, admittedly, on this occasion, Stanhope had done it a bit grudgingly. The Reverend had no idea why the Earl had been so Friday faced about the idea of him and Agnes accompanying Mercedes to Scotland. It wasn't as if the chit was straight out of the schoolroom. Oh, he liked Mercy well enough, but shy and retiring she was not. In truth, she was a Shackleford in all but blood - likely it was her early introduction to Prudence...

Pushing the thoughts of Mercedes out of his mind, he turned his attention back to his stomach. Come to think of it, he was feeling a little peckish. Perhaps he would venture downstairs and ask for some bread and cheese. With a bit of luck, Agnes would already be well into her afternoon nap. A nice ripe stilton would go very well with his brandy...

***

Seating herself at a small desk in her bedchamber, Mercedes endeavoured to put the image of the disfigured man out of her mind. Likely, she would never see him again. Indeed, given the horrific nature of his scar, why would she wish to?

Pulling a sheet of writing parchment to her, Mercy took up her quill. Minutes later, she sighed and put it down again. She'd been intending to pen a letter to her friend Victoria, but the words simply wouldn't come, despite having so much news to impart. Instead, her mind kept replaying the moment the mysterious man had realised she was watching him. The sardonic twist of his lips and the barest, almost contemptuous nod of his head. What was it about him? She imagined he might well have been handsome before his injury.

Leaning back in her chair, she pondered what could have caused such a terrible wound. He didn't look old enough to have fought in the Peninsular Wars.

Bizarrely, she found herself wondering what colour his eyes were, whether his lips were really as full as they appeared from a distance. Suddenly restless, she got to her feet and went back to the window, staring down into the now empty courtyard. Would he be at dinner this evening? Somehow, she didn't think so. Even in the short time she'd watched him, she could tell he wore his loneliness like a shroud.

She shook her head impatiently and stepped away from the window. Why the devil should she care whether some wanderer made an appearance? The man was nothing to her - she had much more pressing issues to consider. Resolutely, she went back to the desk, determined to finish her letter before dinner.

***

The Reverend took a sip of his brandy and followed it with the last piece of stilton, closing his eyes, better to enjoy the sharp tanginess of the cheese together with the sweetness of the brandy. As the Almighty in his wisdom understood so well, it was the little things that made life worthwhile.

When he'd come down to the bar earlier, he'd been the only patron, but now the room was more than half full. He glanced down at his pocket watch – there was still a good couple of hours before dinner. If he returned to his bedchamber now, there'd still be enough time for a bit of a nap. Finishing the last of his brandy, he began to push back his chair, only to stop as a large torso abruptly appeared in front of him.

Heart sinking, the Reverend's eyes travelled upwards until he was staring into the saturnine features of a stranger who looked as though he'd just walked out of a gambling den. 'May I help you, my good man?' he queried, his heart undeniably sinking.

'Would I be right in thinking you a pastor?' The man's voice was deep, and his accent suggested he came from the Americas.

'Indeed, I am,' Reverend Shackleford responded, his interest piqued. 'If I'm not mistaken, you're a long way from home, my friend.' He ignored Flossy's sudden stiffening on his lap, followed by a low growl.

'And not likely to return anytime soon,' the man responded with a heavy sigh 'May I join you for a moment? I have something that's been troubling me that I'm hoping a man of your persuasion might be able to help me with. It should not take long.'

The Reverend swallowed a grimace, instead plastering what he hoped was a welcoming smile on his face. Any chance of a nap was disappearing faster than he could say forty winks. But then, he was God's representative on earth and all that. The Almighty was just reminding him of that. Mayhap he'd enjoyed the cheese a little too much.

With an internal sigh, he waved at the vacant chair. 'I am here to serve. May I be so bold as to ask your name?' He hurriedly stroked Flossy's head as her grumbles got louder.

'Reinhardt,' the man responded as he sat down. 'Oliver Reinhardt. With a hidden *d*.'

The Reverend raised his eyebrows slightly. 'Reverend Augustus Shackleford at your service, Mr. Reinhardt. From your accent I'd taken you from the Americas, but perhaps I was mistaken.'

His companion gave a tight smile. 'My parents emigrated to Boston when I was still a babe. They came originally from

Alsace.'

'Ah.' The Reverend nodded politely and waited.

'Do you perform marriages perchance?'

Reverend Shackleford blinked. Truly the man's words were the last thing he'd expected. 'You have a young lady you wish to wed?' he questioned. The man nodded without expounding.

'I'm afraid I must ask. Do you have her parent's consent?' the Reverend probed.

Reinhardt's eyes narrowed a little, then he sighed and spread his hands. 'I am from Boston. Naturally, her parents do not wish to see their daughter taken so far away. But my love is determined to become my wife if a pastor can be found to marry us. I have obtained the required special licence.'

The Reverend frowned. The whole business was beginning to sound extremely havey-cavey. 'I'm afraid I cannot be a party, however small, to helping a young lady wed against her parent's wishes,' he finally responded carefully.

An uncomfortable silence ensued, until at length, Reinhardt gave a light laugh. 'I was hoping that a man of the cloth might give at least the smallest consideration to true love. But I should have known better. In America, we don't have your stilted values. Back in Boston, it is common to marry for love.'

He pushed back his chair and stood up, inclining his head slightly. 'Thank you for your time. I will leave you to your peaceful contemplation.'

And with that he strode away, leaving Reverend Shackleford staring after him in disquiet.

Chapter Three

Nate ate two-thirds of his stew before putting the bowl down for Ruby to finish. He was seated on the stable floor next to Duchess after creating himself a makeshift bed out of the relatively clean straw. It was almost dark in the stall, reducing the objects around him to vague shapes. The half door to the courtyard was shut, but still the wintery weather crept under the gap, blowing a frigid wind across his back.

At times like this, his scar ached like the devil, and he had to fight the urge to claw at his face as though doing so would somehow stretch the puckered skin. While Ruby noisily licked around the bowl, he pulled down his scarf and rubbed at his cheek, wincing as he pressed his fingers into the old wound. Unexpectedly, the memory of fingers, much gentler than his, tracing the scar, gently rubbing a healing salve across the inflamed skin came into his head. He'd been told that the unguent was the reason the wound had remained free of infection - the reason he'd actually survived.

Catching his breath, Nate dragged his attention back to the present before he was lost in the recurring nightmare of that day. Heart thudding, his mind sought something, *anything* to break the grip of the past. He felt himself slipping, slipping … until abruptly, the image of a woman's face through a window halted the onslaught.

He became aware that Ruby was nosing his hand, whining

anxiously. Taking a deep breath, he pulled the little dog to him and leaned down to kiss the top of her silky head as his thoughts grasped the lifeline that had been offered.

Who was she? The only thing he'd been able to discern clearly through the window was the colour of her hair – as black as a raven's wing. But still he'd known the minute she caught sight of his scar. He'd waited for her to turn away in disgust, but she hadn't. Her hand had come up to the windowpane, almost in a gesture of sympathy, as she continued to watch him solemnly.

For some reason, he found himself wishing fervently that he'd seen her face clearly. He couldn't remember the last time he'd looked at someone – really *looked*. Then with a grimace, he shook his head. What was he – some kind of goat to ogle her so? He shook off his idiocy and picked up the empty bowl, intending to return it to the kitchen while giving Ruby a last opportunity to do her business before they both bedded down for the night.

He was just about to get to his feet, when suddenly the door was pulled open. Instinctively, he sank back into the straw, invisible behind Duchess's flank, watching between her legs as two pairs of feet entered the stable. Beside him, Ruby gave a low, warning growl and Nate laid his hand gently on her head to quieten her.

'She's travellin' wi' a couple o' relatives – one of 'em's a priest.'

There was a short bark of laughter. 'I think I spoke to him earlier. Any bodyguards?' Unlike the first voice, this one was cultured, albeit with an accent implying the speaker wasn't English.

'Five wi' the two coachmen. If yer plannin' on takin' 'er, you best make sure they don't get a look at yer face.'

'Dead witnesses can't tell any tales.' Nate caught his breath at the casual callousness. Were they planning an abduction of some kind? Clearly, they were looking for a young, gently bred female. Abruptly, the woman with the midnight hair came into his mind.

'But what about the priest? He might do the deed wi' the right persuasion.'

'If he's a relative, no amount of coin will convince him to marry the chit against her will.' The voice gave a dark chuckle. 'And there was I, thinking a pastor had been handed to me on a plate – a quick ceremony, then straight down to Plymouth. We could have caught an earlier ship...'

The voice paused and uttered a soft expletive before continuing. 'No, the plan stands. I'll drag her whining arse to Salisbury. I have another priest there ready and waiting, and it will only waste another two or three days. We'll still be leaving this cursed island a lot earlier than if we'd waited to snatch her in London.' There was another pause, and for a second Nate thought they were about to leave, then the cultured voice continued.

'About two miles past Corsham, there's a copse of trees. We'll wait for them there. In the meantime, make sure Smith and the others don't drink themselves under the bloody table. We'll meet here at dawn.'

The door opened, and seconds later they were gone. Nate swore softly to himself, running his fingers through his unkempt hair. So much for keeping himself to himself. Should he put the conversation out of his mind? After all, many would say it was none of his bloody business if some fellow thought to marry a woman against her will. That kind of thing happened all the time. The man must be a fortune hunter which meant the girl had to come from a wealthy family - considerably wealthy considering the lengths he was prepared to go, up to and including murder...

Could he live with himself if he ignored the woman's plight? He had a pistol, but he'd be no match for a group of hardened criminals. He glanced up at Duchess. The mare was in no fit state to go gallivanting round the countryside, so clearly the answer wasn't galloping to the damsel's rescue like some erstwhile knight in shining armour. Whatever he did would have to be done this night. And he didn't even know which deuced woman they were after.

There were enough clues though. The woman was evidently a lady, and he'd overheard the kidnappers say she was travelling with a priest. That knowledge alone should be enough to discover her identity. If he could convince both her and her companions that they were in danger – that they needed to leave the inn as soon as possible without being seen... Nate bit back a humourless laugh. What was the likelihood of them believing anything that came out of his mouth?

And where the hell would they go?

'*Shit.*' He sighed and shut his eyes. He'd have to take them to Carlingford Hall. *If* he could convince them to leave.

With another sigh, he climbed stiffly to his feet. First things first. He hadn't got a look at either of the speakers, but he'd recognise their voices if he heard them again. If either of them was in the dining room, he'd know. Sadly, his appearance would attract attention, but there was nothing he could do about that.

He brushed the straw off his breeches and boots, then tidied his hair, retying the queue. Lastly, he took off his great coat, tucked in his shirt and straightened the cravat at his neck. There was no use in covering the scar. If he attempted to walk into the dining room with his face covered, he'd likely be thrown out on his ear within minutes. He gave a dark chuckle. They might do that anyway once the landlord got a look at his ruined face.

After giving Duchess a last scratch, he made sure she had plenty of fodder, and went out into the cold, Ruby at his heels.

***

Unsurprisingly, with the inclement weather, the dining room was very busy, and Mercy was glad her father had booked a private room. Usually she enjoyed being around people, but tonight she was tired. Though not particularly arduous, the journey had been long, and she'd spent most of it in her own head. She was weary, and not just in body.

Fortunately, the private dining room was cosy and warm thanks to a large fire crackling in the hearth, and as Mercy waited for her companions, she thought back to the letter she'd sent to Victoria. In the end, it was nearly six pages long – almost a novel.

She and Jennifer had met Victoria following Anthony Shackleford's marriage to Tory's twin sister Georgiana. Though the circumstances of their meeting were particularly extraordinary, the three had since become firm friends, attending their first two seasons together. To date, only Jennifer had found her soulmate, though it had happened about as far from the *ton* marriage mart as one could get.

Originally, Tory had intended to accompany Mercy to Caerlaverock, but with the unexpected early arrival of George's first child, she correctly surmised her help would be needed and elected to go and stay with her sister and Anthony instead.

Mercy was well aware that her friend was every bit as weary of the strutting peacocks parading round the ballrooms of London, but unlike Mercy, if she chose not to undertake another season, she could simply refuse.

As the granddaughter of the late Earl of Rutledge, and through a complex twist of fate, Victoria was in full control of her inheritance and could do as she wished. Mercy felt a momentary pang of envy. Oh, to have that kind of freedom. Then she took herself to task. Her father was no ogre and would never force her to do anything she really didn't want. And she knew that Tory had spent so much of her life alone. Only discovering she had a twin sister and subsequently being taken under the wing of the Duke and Duchess of Blackmore had saved her from becoming a complete recluse.

Tory hadn't yet decided whether to do another season. Indeed, Mercy had a suspicion that she might simply remain with her sister and travel with her to Blackmore for the Duke and Duchess's house party in July. Mercy had been invited of course, being the stepdaughter of one of the Duchess's sisters, and she assumed the rest of the Shackleford clan, together with their spouses and offspring would likely be there. Even Jennifer was hoping to make the journey from Scotland. Mercy was looking forward to it immensely and not simply because it would give her an excuse to leave London.

And who knew? There was always the outside chance she would meet the man of her dreams in Blackmore. Though their invitations were widely sought after, both Nicholas and Grace were notoriously particular about who they asked into their home. At the very least, their guest list was never boring.

All Mercy had to do was get through the next two and a half months. And really, who was going to be interested in a spinster on her third season?

The sudden crackling of the fire interrupted her reverie, and just as she realised the room was beginning to get uncomfortably hot, the door opened abruptly, admitting Flossy who promptly came charging across the room to throw herself into Mercy's lap.

'Tare an' hounds,' the Reverend groaned, stomping in behind the little dog, 'It's hotter than Satan's ear wax in here.'

'Nonsense, Augustus,' countered Agnes, seating herself at the table. 'I instructed them to stoke up the fire.' The matron nodded in satisfaction at the roaring flames, now in danger of setting fire to anything within a ten-yard radius. 'Naturally, I did not want to risk getting an ague in this unseasonal weather.'

The Reverend mopped at his brow 'I don't know about an ague, I'll be done to a crisp just in time for dinner, the only thing missing'll be a deuced apple between me teeth.'

'I doubt the fire will continue to burn so vigorously for much longer,' Mercy predicted, fanning her perspiring face. 'And anyway, I'm confident the innkeeper will be here directly.'

'I certainly hope so,' Agnes declared, 'I'd risk a cropping for a large sweet sherry.'

***

On entering the bar and dining room, Nate made sure to keep his back to the candles as much as he could. The room was almost full, with most of the patrons already eating. Hanging back by the door, he searched the room for a young well-dressed woman and a priest. After a few minutes his heart sank. There was nobody in the room even remotely fitting that description.

His eyes roamed the area again as he weighed his options. He couldn't very well search every bedchamber, so if they'd been and gone or didn't come down to dinner at all, his only recourse would be to watch for them in the morning when likely he wouldn't be the only one. Any attempt he made to get them to safety would be doomed before he'd even tried. To make matters worse, there were several well-dressed gentlemen in the room – any one of them might be the would-be abductor and would be sure to notice any interaction. Nate gritted his teeth in frustration, tempted to wash his hands of the whole smoky business.

After a few more seconds deliberation, he stepped away from the door, and strode over to the bar, Ruby at his heels. A tankard of ale would at least give him a legitimate reason to be there. The barmaid eyed his scar as she poured, but otherwise made no comment.

Nodding his thanks, Nate took his pint to a small empty table in the corner and prepared to wait. After about twenty minutes, he noticed a serving girl carrying a tray laden with food out of the dining room and into a narrow passageway. When she came back a couple of minutes later, the tray was empty. Clearly, she was taking the food somewhere. Moments later the innkeeper went the same way carrying a tankard of ale and what looked like two glasses of sherry.

One man and two women? That made sense. Gently bred ladies did not usually travel without another female chaperone. Feeling a rising sense of apprehension mixed with relief, Nate watched for a little while longer. Were they eating in their bedchambers? As far as he could tell, the passageway also led to the stairs. But no, it would have taken a lot longer to take the food and drink all the way upstairs. There had to be a private room.

Could he access it without the occupants screaming the place down the moment he went through the door? He took a sip of his pint and glanced round the room. No one appeared to be paying him any attention. The candlelight cast people-shaped shadows on the wall, creating an almost dreamlike atmosphere and turning his disfigurement into a prop from a mummers play. It was now or never.

Casually, Nate finished his pint and rose to his feet. He didn't have to tell Ruby to stay with him as he sauntered casually towards the passageway, trying to look as if he had every right to be there. If it had been daytime, he would have stuck out like a sore thumb, but as far as he could tell, no one even glanced his way.

Once he'd entered the passageway and was out of sight of the diners, he paused to get his bearings. After a few yards, the narrow corridor opened up into a square hallway with a set of stairs disappearing up into the gloom. There were two doors. Glancing back behind him, Nate strode quickly to the first one and listened. There was no noise coming from the other side. Cautiously, he pushed open the door. The room beyond was dark and clearly empty. He shut the door again and moved to the next one, inclining his head to listen. For a second he thought he'd been wrong, but then he heard voices.

Heart thudding, he took a deep breath and pushed open the door.

Chapter Four

Thankfully, the fire didn't continue to rage, and Mercy couldn't help breathing a sigh of relief once she was no longer afraid it might burn the whole inn down with them in it.

Their dinner, when it finally arrived, consisted of a bowl containing what the serving girl described as, '*cock wi gin.*' For once the Reverend appeared lost for words while Agnes immediately began rummaging in her reticule for her salts. Looking down at her plate, Mercy simply hoped it was chicken swimming in the dark gravy.

Despite the unpromising start however, the food turned out to be surprisingly tasty and before long all three of them were tucking in happily. A few minutes later, the innkeeper himself came in with their drinks, and Agnes benevolently pronounced the sherry *passable* using the nasally twang she typically reserved for tradesmen and Percy Noon's mother, Mary.

Mercy was just contemplating whether a hunk of bread to mop up the juices would be too unladylike, when, without warning, the door was pushed open again. Looking up in surprise, any other retort she might have made died in her throat. It was the scarred man she'd seen from the window. Her heart thudded with a mixture of fear and … something else, but before she had the chance to examine it, Flossy caught sight of the small terrier at the man's heels and set up a cacophony of barking.

To her alarm, the man ordered his dog inside and promptly shut the door while Reverend Shackleford hurriedly tossed his napkin onto the table and stood up. 'What the devil do you think you're doing?' he blustered.

The man stepped forward, holding out his hands in an unmistakeable gesture of conciliation. 'Before you shout for help, I beg you to listen.' His voice was unquestionably cultured, but as he stepped into the candlelight, the shadows made his face look almost demonic. A second later, Agnes gave a small moan before sliding slowly off her chair, landing on the floor with a loud thud.

'Grandmama!' Mercy gasped, jumping up and hurrying round to the matron. Raising her skirt, she got onto her hands and knees, completely forgetting about the man for a moment.

After a few seconds, Agnes's eyes fluttered open. 'Salts,' she croaked, raising a limp hand.

'Here they are, my dove.' For a second, Mercy wondered who the Reverend was talking to until the small bottle was held out in front of her.

Taking it from him, she held it near to the matron's nose, wafting it gently.

'Thunder an' turf, even Flossy wouldn't smell that,' the Reverend declared after a second. 'Here, give it to me.' Laboriously he got down onto the floor as Mercy obligingly handed him the bottle and sat back on her heels to give him room, only to watch incredulously as he practically stuffed the bottle up his wife's nose. However, it appeared to do the trick and after a couple of seconds, Agnes came round enough to ask if there was any more sherry.

Relieved, Mercy helped the Reverend get the matron back into her chair, suddenly catching sight of the reason Agnes had fainted in the first place. For a few seconds, she'd forgotten he was there. To her surprise, Flossy had ceased her barking and was now busy getting acquainted with the newcomers. The little dog could usually be relied upon to determine whether a stranger was trustworthy or not, and the fact that she was busy capering around the man's ankles automatically lessened Mercy's fear. Evidently, it had the same effect on the Reverend who seemed content to leave her to deal with the stranger as he gave Agnes the remnants of her sherry.

'Who are you?' Mercy asked him, pleased to note that her voice was only wobbling a little.

'Nathaniel Harding, at your service, my lady.' He took off his hat and gave a small inclination of his head.

'And do you make a habit of sneaking into private dining rooms, Mr. Harding?'

He gave a rueful smile, and for some reason, even though the scar twisted his lips, Mercy's heart thudded - and not in fear. 'I've come here to tell you that I believe someone at the inn means you harm.'

His voice was pleasantly deep with a rich timbre. Almost soporific. 'But that someone is not you?' she questioned, raising her eyebrows.

He shook his head impatiently. 'I implore you to listen to what I have to say, my lady.' He turned his attention to encompass the Reverend and a now frowning Agnes, 'I truly believe that all three of you are in grave danger.' Taking a deep breath, he told them what he'd overheard in the stable. 'I have no way of knowing for sure that you are their intended victim,' he finished, turning back to Mercy, 'but to my knowledge, there's no other young lady staying here in the company of a priest.'

There was a disbelieving silence until the Reverend growled, 'I'm a vicar, not a priest.'

'And you say this man means to abduct me with the aim of forcing me into wedlock? With him presumably?'

Nate nodded his head, wondering at her continued composure – in his experience, most women would, at the very least, have burst into tears. 'It sounds preposterous, but I can assure you that's exactly what I overheard.' He turned to the Reverend. 'I believe he meant it when he said he would leave no witnesses.'

'But why me?' Mercy quizzed. 'I mean, what could he possibly hope to gain?'

Nate shrugged. 'I have no idea, I presumed he was a fortune hunter. In truth, I don't even know what he looks like, though I don't think he was English. His accent sounded like he was from the Americas.'

'Tare an' hounds, I think I actually spoke to him,' the Reverend interjected suddenly. 'A suspicious looking individual approached me in the bar earlier. Asked about marrying some young lady without her parent's consent. I thought it all sounded deuced havey-cavey and told him in no uncertain terms that I'd never conduct a clandestine wedding.' He shook his head and gave a grimace. 'I had to hold Flossy back. I'd no deuced idea he was talking about you, Mercedes.'

'What did he look like?' Nate asked urgently.

'Swarthy – very foreign looking. Said his name was Oliver Reinhardt, but if he's the blackguard after Mercy, I doubt that's his real name.' The Reverend paused. 'As you said, he had an American accent.'

'I take it you'd remember him if you ever saw him again?' Nate asked grimly.

Reverend Shackleford nodded. 'He had a face one was unlikely to forget easily – a bit like yours really.'

'Grandfather!' Mercy spluttered.

'He had a scar you mean?' Nate interrupted, seemingly unoffended.

The Reverend nodded again. 'Not nearly as bad as yours though. Looked as though he'd had it a long time. It was across his forehead and mostly covered by his hair. I only saw it as he got up to leave.'

Nate nodded. 'Being able to recognise your adversary is half the battle.'

'That as may be,' the Reverend acknowledged, 'but exactly what would you have us do? We can hardly run in the middle of the night.'

'That's exactly what I believe you should do,' Nate returned, ignoring the three incredulous stares. 'Quietly and in secret. This Reinhardt - if indeed that's his name - and his cohorts will not be looking for you until the morning. By then, you could be away from here and safe.'

'And what about the carriage, and my clothes?'

Agnes's voice was shrill, and she was waving her salts around as though she was about to fall off the chair again any second. Clearly, Nate thought, she didn't share the younger woman's fortitude.

'And where would we go?' Mercy demanded. 'I am hardly dressed for a hike in the snow. We'd likely freeze to death before we find shelter.'

Nate shut his eyes for a second, deliberating how to phrase his proposed solution without being summarily dismissed. In the end, he simply shrugged and said, 'My house is close. I could take you there until the danger has passed.'

'Are you addled?' the Reverend scoffed. 'Do you really think we are bottle headed enough to abandon all our belongings and accompany you to your house in the middle of the night?'

Nate gave the clergyman a level stare. 'It matters not to me,' he said at length. 'Accept my offer of help or don't. It's not my life that's in danger. Should you decide to remain here, I will simply return to the stable and bed down with my horse for the night.' He gave a shrug. 'Take your chances tomorrow, Sir, if that's what you prefer to do.'

'How do we know you won't simply rob us and leave us for dead?' Mercy pressed.

'You don't,' was his short answer. 'But if you recall, I suggested you leave your belongings.'

'You may have an accomplice ready and waiting to go through our things,' Agnes protested.

'I might,' Nate returned, 'but I don't know anything about you, including which bedchambers you are sleeping in.'

'So you say,' Agnes retorted darkly.

Nate ran his hands through his hair in frustration. 'We are running out of time,' he bit out. 'I repeat, it is of no moment to me whether you stay here or come with me. I'm not exactly relishing the thought of a midnight stroll in the snow.'

'I thought you said you had a horse?' Mercy quizzed.

'She took a stone to her shoe earlier today. That's why I'm here. She will be rested enough to get home, but not to ride.'

'How far is your house?'

'I estimate it will probably take us an hour if we keep up a reasonable pace.'

'We have two coach drivers and three footmen attending us. What do we tell them?' Mercy pressed.

Nate raised his eyebrows. 'Do you always travel in such numbers?'

'We have just returned from Scotland. They are for our protection.'

'Exactly,' the Reverend declared triumphantly. 'Our *protection*. I'm certain they'll be more than a match for a bunch of murdering guttersnipes.'

There was a pause, then Nate sighed. 'So, you've made your decision then?'

'We have,' the Reverend answered firmly.

Nate nodded slowly. 'Very well. Tell your protectors the varmints intend to wait in a copse of trees on the other side of Corsham. I assume that *is* your direction?'

Mercy nodded uncertainly.

'Mayhap we'll take another route,' the Reverend announced defensively.

'I'm not sure it will make a difference. They will be watching for your rising,' Nate answered. 'I overheard the man telling his accomplice to meet outside the stables at dawn.'

'Will you still be here at that time?' Mercy asked hesitantly.

'I will be here until just before dawn. I want to get Duchess to the comfort of her own stable as soon as possible…' He paused, and for a second, Mercy thought he was about to add something significant, but in the end, all he said was, 'I wish you all Godspeed.'

Then, replacing his hat, he tapped his thigh to summon his dog, who was curled up by the fire with Flossy, and seconds later he was gone.

***

Mercedes turned over and thumped at her pillow as sleep continued to elude her. Indeed, she didn't think she'd ever felt more awake in her life. The events of the evening kept going round and round in her head until she thought she would scream.

Despite the gravity of his message, all Mercy could think about was *him*. Nathaniel Harding. As soon as he left the room, she'd felt bereft, as though she'd lost something incredibly important. She realised that after his initial entrance, she'd stopped seeing the scar on his face entirely - and just thinking about the rich timbre of his voice unaccountably made her squirm.

She understood the Reverend's mistrust. What did they know of him really? But for some reason, Mercy would willingly have trusted him with her life. She would have gone with him without a backward glance.

But she couldn't argue with her step-grandfather's logic - he was responsible for her. And whilst the idea of Augustus Shackleford being responsible for anything or anyone other than himself would have most of his offspring falling over laughing, the truth was, he'd taken his duty to her seriously. At least on the journey there and back at any rate. While at Caerlaverock she could have fallen into the loch or been abducted by a dozen would-be ravishers, and he wouldn't have known about it until dinner.

Mercy sighed in the dark. As the Reverend had said, 'Forewarned is forearmed.' Now that they knew about a potential attack, they could take the appropriate steps. And the *footmen* accompanying them were retired sailors recruited and trained by the Duke of Blackmore specifically to provide protection on long journeys. They would know exactly what to do.

Determinedly, she turned over onto her side and closed her eyes. It would do no good to lie awake all night.

Seconds later, she was on her back again. It was *her* presence that was putting everyone in danger. If she wasn't there, and the blackguard who had designs on her knew it, he would leave her companions alone. She sat up, forcing down the sudden spurt of terror at being the actual target of a kidnapping attempt. What if *she* went into hiding with Nathaniel Harding?

On her own?

Swallowing, she climbed out of bed and hurried to the window. How long was it before dawn? She felt as though she'd been tossing and turning for hours, but the full moon told her it was likely a couple of hours yet to sunrise. She sat down on the edge of the bed. The sensible part of her knew her idea was completely totty-headed. Mercedes did not have the recklessness of the rest of the Shackleford family – which wasn't entirely surprising since they weren't actually her blood relatives. Indeed, her insistence on visiting Jennifer was the first time she and her father had really had an altercation.

That dispute, however, had served to prove that she wasn't completely immune to the general wildness exhibited by her adopted family, and was perfectly capable of digging her heels in when the mood took her - though, it had to be said her father hadn't seemed quite so thrilled by the abrupt appearance of such a Shackleford trait...

Mercy nibbled anxiously at her fingernails. She could leave a note for her step-grandparents explaining her reasoning. Granted, as soon as her father read it, he might well throw his father-in-law out on his ear, but better that than attending the clergyman's funeral.

She forced down another surge of fear. Could Mr. Harding be trusted? What if she was jumping from the frying pan into the fire? Then she thought of Flossy's reaction to him. She had never known the little dog to be wrong in her assessment of people. Never.

And Flossy had trusted him.

Without giving herself further time to dither, Mercy hurriedly took off her nightgown and put on her warmest day dress. Fortunately, she'd taken her sensible boots to Scotland in anticipation of getting plenty of exercise. Then she made up a small bag of essentials, reasoning that either Mr. Harding or his horse would be able to carry it. It was unlikely she'd have to remain in hiding for long – simply long enough for the Reverend to get to Cottesmore. She had no doubt her father would tear the countryside apart to find her.

Finally, after writing a quick note to her grandfather, she picked up her cloak, and tiptoed to the door, only to pause before she turned the knob.

Was Mr. Harding married? He hadn't mentioned a wife, and somehow, she couldn't imagine him leg shackled – he appeared too … solitary. And then there was the scar.

So, what about a chaperone? Mercy frowned, hesitating on the threshold. Did he have servants? Then she took herself to task. What the deuce was she doing, worrying about proprieties when people's lives were in danger? Only her closest family and Mr. Harding himself would ever know that she stayed there, and it wouldn't be for long – perhaps two days at the most. She pursed her lips and pulled open the door.

Seconds later she was creeping down the stairs and along the passageway in the direction of the stables.

Chapter Five

Settling himself back on his makeshift bed in the stable, Nate expected to feel relief that the young woman and her companions had rejected his offer of succour. He'd done his duty and as a result, their chances of foiling the kidnap attempt on the morrow were much improved.

Unfortunately, in his head, he kept seeing a pair of soft brown eyes, olive skin and coal black hair. What did the Reverend call her? Mercy, that was it. A strange name. Mayhap it was short for something. He thought for a second. She had a very Spanish look about her so it could be her name was Mercedes. It was a fairly common name in Spain, and one he'd come across many times during his time with Wellington.

But then, if she was Spanish, how did she have an English grandmother? No, her accent was definitely English – and cultured. She was gently bred; of that he was certain. Not only did she sound it, but her dress was clearly of good quality and why else would someone wish to kidnap and wed her against her will?

And then there was the clergyman – was he any relation? Why had she been in Scotland? How the devil had she become the target of a bloody kidnapper? The questions went round and round in his head, thwarting any attempt to sleep.

He had no doubt she'd been the woman in the window. The one

who'd intrigued him even then. Could he truly just leave her to her fate?

He swore under his breath, pillowing his head in his arms. Duchess whickered softly while Ruby snuggled closer to him. The two animals were his only friends. There was literally no one else. How had he become so isolated? Almost as if in answer, his scar throbbed dully. Even after all these years, there were still times when the whole side of his face ached like the devil.

Groaning, he started to turn over, when suddenly he heard a noise. Ruby lifted her head, growling softly. Slowly, carefully, Nate sat up, feeling underneath the straw for his hidden pistol. As the stable door began to open, he rose quietly to his feet, stepping around Duchess to face the intruder. There would be no hiding this time.

Seconds later, the door was pushed fully open, and Nate's breath huffed out in disbelief as a feminine head leaned hesitantly through. 'Mr. Harding...?' She stepped into the stable, squinting into the dim light cast by the lone lantern hanging high in the rafters for safety. 'Mr. Harding, are you there?' Her voice was a hoarse whisper.

What the devil was she doing here unaccompanied in the middle of the night? He moved forward into the light, his voice coming out harsher than he'd intended. 'Are you alone?'

She visibly jumped and took an involuntary step backwards. 'I... I...' she stammered, before seemingly taking herself to task and straightening her spine. 'I have come to accept your offer of assistance,' she declared, holding her chin up.

Clearly, there was no one with her. The foolish chit really had come alone.

'Do your companions know you are here?' Nate asked, making an effort to soften his voice.

'I… I've left them a note.' She took a step towards him and held out her hand in supplication. 'I am the one this blackguard is looking for. They will be safe as long as I'm not with them.'

Silence ensued as Nate assimilated her words. He couldn't argue with her logic. 'Where are you travelling to?'

'Cottesmore,' she returned promptly. 'It's near to Ringwood in the New Forest.'

'I know it,' he answered, then frowned. 'Is your father the Earl?'

Mercy simply nodded and Nate gave a low whistle. 'That explains the kidnapping attempt.' He shook his head. 'And am I likely to survive a confrontation with your father once he learns we have spent time alone together?'

'Don't you have any servants?' she asked in a small voice.

Nate shook his head. 'Alas, my coffers do not extend to hired help.' He quirked a mocking brow and added, 'Come to think of it, mayhap Reinhardt's plan does have merit.' He watched her face suffuse with colour, wondering why he was provoking her. Looking at her beautiful, *refined* face, he realised that deep down, in that secret place where all his resentment festered, he was angry – furious in fact.

A bloody abduction attempt. That was what it took to get a woman to visit his home. His anger was completely irrational. He couldn't actually remember the last time he'd even invited a female to Carlingford Hall, let alone a lady.

She took a step back, and Nate could see she was on the verge of bolting. Angry at himself now, he held up a conciliatory hand. 'You have nothing to fear from me,' he said gruffly. 'Just my twisted sense of humour, I'm afraid.'

She bit her lip but came no closer, and he could see she was clutching her cloth bag in a death grip.

'I will keep you safe,' he added softly. 'I swear it. Until your father gets here. I will not allow any harm to come to you.'

For long seconds, she simply stared at him, then abruptly nodded her head. Once. It was enough. The relief engulfing Nate at that smallest of nods was so shocking in its intensity, he almost sagged against Duchess's flank. What the hell? A small whine at his feet brought him back to the situation, and mentally shaking himself, he bent to fuss Ruby, then began to saddle the mare.

'I think since we are going to be sharing the same four walls, it would be appropriate to ask your name?' he declared over his shoulder as he heaved the saddle onto the horse's back, 'or at least what you'd prefer me to call you.'

He heard her step towards him. 'It's Mercedes – Mercy for short,' was the small answer.

He turned round in surprise. 'You'll allow me to use your first name?' He watched as her face coloured up for the second time, evidently realising her faux pas. Then she sighed and shrugged.

'These are hardly normal circumstances. Should the world discover that I spent time with a man alone in his house, then your use of my first name will be the least of my worries.'

'Better that than forced to wed a murdering bastard,' he countered with a tight grin.

'Succinctly put,' she agreed with a small smile of her own.

'No one will find out,' he vowed, tightening the girth. 'We do not mix in the same circles my lady...' He paused, giving a small chuckle. 'In truth, I don't mix in any circles.' He cast a droll look behind him. 'I'm like the beast in the fairytale.'

'You've read Beauty and the Beast?' she asked in surprise.

'Who hasn't?' he countered, taking her bag. 'I thought it was requisite reading for all children. Parents the world over love a good morality tale.'

'So do you have the good heart and generous spirit of the prince, then?' she quizzed, stepping up beside him and stroking the mare's flank.

Absurdly irritated that she'd referred to the beast's character rather than his ugliness, Nate ignored her question, instead saying flatly, 'Her name's Duchess. Be careful; she bites.' He shoved down the petty satisfaction of watching her step back a little and picked up the panniers containing his provisions, throwing them over the horse's back. 'We should have enough food for three days – four if we are careful. Unfortunately, it will not be the kind of fare you're no doubt accustomed to.'

'You have no idea what I'm accustomed to,' Mercy retorted tartly, handing him her bag. 'Do not make the mistake of thinking me a ninnyhammer, Mr. Harding.'

He cast her a wry look. 'I stand corrected. And it's Nate. As you say, we are well beyond the boundaries of propriety.' He took hold of the horse's reins. 'I'll lead Duchess out of the stables, keeping to the side closest to the inn. If you walk on her other side and keep your head bowed, you will hopefully be lost to the shadows. There is nothing we can do about the sound of her hoofs on the cobbles. The snow should muffle it a little.'

Mercy bit her lip and nodded her head, pulling up her cloak hood to hide her face. Nate clicked his tongue, urging the mare forward. Ruby was already at the door, tail wagging in enthusiasm. Watching the little terrier's excitement reminded her of Flossy, lessening her fear a little. As they stepped outside, she resisted a senseless urge to look up at the darkened windows, and kept close to the horse's side, her head bowed, while they made their slow, tortuous way across the courtyard.

Two minutes later, they were out onto the deserted road. Little did she know that her life would never be the same again.

Chapter Six

The Reverend woke early, though in truth, he wasn't really sure he'd actually been asleep.

It wasn't often Augustus Shackleford questioned his own decisions. Introspection wasn't generally something he indulged in since it tended to bring on his gout. And for the most part, he believed that if a course of action came to him, it had been put there by the Almighty. For that reason, it was perfectly acceptable for him to go along with it – though, in fairness, there had been the odd occasion where he had to admit (mostly after the event) that he may just have *slightly* misconstrued His meaning.

This could well be one of those occasions.

If he was being entirely honest, he felt completely out of his depth. Despite his determined words the evening before, he wasn't entirely sure their *footmen* were capable of protecting them against what were essentially a bunch of murdering land pirates.

And at the end of the day, he had no real idea why this American was looking to abduct Mercedes. The man had implied that he'd only recently come to England from the Americas. It was a deuced long way to come simply to force a chit's hand in marriage to get his hands on her dowry. And how had he come to know about her anyway?

And lastly, the most important thing. The one that had been nagging him since he climbed into bed. Christian Stanhope, Earl of Cottesmore, had lived in America for several years before returning to England to claim his inheritance.

At the time of his leaving, he'd been living in New York City, but before that, Augustus Shackleford knew his son-in-law had spent several years in the very same place as Reinhardt.

Boston, Massachusetts.

***

Christian Stanhope watched Christopher, Olivia and Catherine - or Kit, Ollie and Kate as they were more commonly known - as they made the most of the unseasonal weather. Though the hour was still early, the twins were currently sat on top of their brother pummelling him with snow. The Earl winced, giving a rueful grin while wondering whether he should intervene.

The girls were entirely too much for his bookish son to fight off alone, though he suspected Kit would not appreciate his father's interference. In truth, when the twins were together, they were almost impossible for anyone to control. What was it about Shackleford women? He shook his head and chuckled to himself. He loved all his children fiercely, but he had to admit to having missed Mercedes this last month. The twins adored her, and whenever Mercy was in the house, they gravitated towards their half-sister, giving the rest of the household a little well-earned respite.

'Have they suffocated him yet?' Christian turned at the sound of Chastity's voice and shook his head with a grin.

'Kit is far too soft on them,' his wife continued, coming to stand at the window to watch the play fight. 'They run rings round him I'm afraid.'

'I'm sensing a common theme with the males in this family,'

Christian retorted drily.

Chastity looked at him and winked. 'We wouldn't want any of you to be bored,' she quipped, then laughed at his answering look. 'Have you heard from Mercy?' she asked, thinking it a good time to change the subject.

'She sent a messenger to say they had left Tewkesbury and were hoping to arrive before dark today. He gestured to the white blanket in front of them. 'Of course, that was before the snow arrived. They might be forced to stay an extra night in the Swan.'

'Oh, I hope not,' Chastity exclaimed. 'I've missed her dreadfully.' She shook her head, 'Along with fearing that some Scottish laird might sweep her off her feet. I don't think I could bear it if she went so far away.'

'Mostly because she's the only one who can control the twins,' Christian gibed.

'That is absolutely not true,' Chastity protested a little too vehemently, before adding with a rueful grin, 'well mayhap just a little... But you know I love her dearly.'

'And she loves you,' Christian responded, taking his wife in his arms. 'In truth, you've been the most wonderful mother to her, and I'll be forever grateful to you.'

'I feel as though she's mine,' Chastity responded simply, leaning forward to kiss him.

'Well, she's certainly got the Shackleford determination to go her own way as we recently discovered,' Christian chuckled. 'I blame it on Prudence.'

'Poor old Pru - being the youngest, she gets the blame for everything. But at least Mercy listens. Unlike our youngest two mischief-makers.'

'Until she doesn't,' Christian grimaced. 'I confess I've been more than a little concerned about her going so far in your father's company.'

Chastity gave an inelegant snort, 'Whatever she may or may not have done will not have been due to his influence. My father's always been excellent at thinking about his own requirements whilst leaving the rest of us to do whatever we wanted.'

Christian raised his eyebrows. 'But what about all his meddling and interference?'

Chastity shrugged. 'I think he always thought of it as damage limitation. And his meddling was usually his way of trying to put things right after whatever disaster had occurred. He was never very good at thinking ahead.'

'I never quite thought of it that way,' her husband admitted with a frown causing Chastity to shake her head and laugh.

'Don't worry about Mercy, darling. She's more than capable of making her own decisions, and at the end of the day, I'm certain she'd never do anything that might cause you to worry...'

***

'She's gone!' The Reverend burst into his wife's bedchamber without knocking, resulting in Agnes only narrowly avoiding shoving her morning tonic up her nose.

'What do you mean? Who's gone where?' the matron demanded, hurriedly putting the bottle down.

'Mercedes,' he roared. 'She's not in her room.' He waved a scrap of paper around. 'She left this.' He sounded on the verge of tears, and Agnes frowned, wondering if he was about to have an apoplexy. She'd never seen her husband so up in the boughs.

'Let me see,' she ordered, holding out her hand for the note. Seconds later, she gave a small moan and fumbled around for her salts.

'Stanhope will never forgive us,' the Reverend groaned. 'I knew I should have taken that fellow's offer of help last eve.'

'She says she's gone with him to ensure our safety,' Agnes countered firmly. 'Surely our best recourse is to get to Cottesmore as soon as possible. If this blackguard is watching us as Mr. Harding suggested, then he'll know Mercy's not in the carriage and will leave us be.'

'Unless he drags us out of the coach and tortures us until we tell him where she is,' the Reverend muttered darkly.

'I hardly think he will go to such great lengths, Augustus,' Agnes declared, though her conviction appeared to be wavering slightly. 'We will warn the footmen and coach drivers, so they'll be on their guard for any attack.'

Slightly mollified, Reverend Shackleford nodded. 'I'll speak with them now. Be ready to leave within the hour.' He shoved the note in his cassock pocket and started towards the door, only to pause and turn back. 'You do think Mercy will be safe with Harding? I mean, he's not likely to … well…'

'Flossy thought so,' Agnes declared stoutly, echoing Mercy's opinion, 'and that's good enough for me.'

'So, you don't think the fellow intends to … to … well, you know … *err* in the way of his breeches?'

Agnes stared at him for a second. 'You mean is he likely to force her into his bed and ravish her?'

The Reverend stared back. 'Have you been reading those deuced periodicals again, Agnes?' The matron went an uncommon shade of pink, but fortunately she was saved from replying by a knock on the door.

'Stay back, Agnes,' the clergyman ordered in the tone of voice he usually reserved for one of Percy's fire and brimstone sermons.

'Here, take this,' Agnes breathed, lifting the large poker from next to the fire and handing it to him.

Grasping the makeshift weapon, Reverend Shackleford tiptoed to the door. 'Who's there?' he demanded, lifting the poker for good measure before dramatically flinging open the door.

The maid on the other side screamed and nearly dropped her tray. 'I was just bringin' the missus 'er chocolate,' she babbled, backing away. 'I swears it, Sir.'

The Reverend put down the poker, feeling four ways a fool. 'I ... er ... there was a bit of a disturbance last night...' It was true, there was – just because he didn't actually hear Mercy doing a runner, didn't make it a plumper.

'My wife and I didn't sleep well...' Half-truth perhaps – he certainly didn't sleep well. In his experience, Agnes usually slept like the dead, and he didn't think the events of last night would be any exception.

'No matter, Sir,' the maid responded cheerfully, stepping past him into the room. 'I know just how noisy the inn can be when it's busy – people coming and going at all hours.'

'Did anyone leave last night?'

'I don't rightly know, Sir. I ain't bin told so.' The maid placed the hot chocolate onto the table and gave a small curtsy. 'Will you be wantin' breakfast?'

Before Agnes could order her customary five course meal as she generally did when someone else was footing the bill, the Reverend shook his head. 'We're leaving as soon as possible. If you could supply us with some bread and cold meats to take with us, that would be most appreciated.'

'With a spot of piccalilli,' Agnes added as the young woman went through the door.' The maid nodded and hurried away.

'Thunder an' turf, if Reinhardt asks around, he's sure to find out Harding left last night,' the Reverend groaned. 'It won't be long before he puts two and two together once he realises Mercy's missing.'

'But why on earth would he link Harding with Mercy?' Agnes scoffed. 'I think you're beginning to believe your own Banbury stories, Augustus Shackleford.'

'That as may be, but we can't discount the possibility. We need to get to the Earl as soon as possible. I'll go and tell the coachmen not to spare the horses.'

***

Mercy woke with a start, and for a few seconds couldn't imagine where she was, then it all came flooding back. Heart sinking, she stared up at the moth-eaten canopy above the bed she was lying in and thought back to the events that had brought her here.

It had taken them just over an hour to reach the house, and though frightened out of her wits, she'd been heartened to watch her would-be rescuer's concern for his horse, even slowing their pace for the mare's comfort. They spoke very little throughout the trek, and already exhausted from her long journey, Mercy had concentrated on putting one foot in front of another. Surprisingly, it hadn't been particularly cold, and she suspected a thaw was already setting in.

In the note she left for her grandfather, Mercy had advised that they continue on to Cottesmore with all speed. She hoped the Reverend had either kept the note with him or put it onto the fire as soon as he'd read it. If Reinhardt got hold of it, he might not know where she'd gone, but at the very least he'd suspect they were on to him.

Then of course, she couldn't help wondering whether the whole business had been blown out of all proportion, or whether Mr.

Harding had even been telling the truth. But what could he have hoped to gain? Did he want money? Mayhap he hoped her father would pay for her safe return – but then, he hadn't even known who her father was until she told him in the stable.

Her thoughts had gone round and round as she'd trudged alongside the horse. Strangely enough, the one thing she hadn't felt was fear of her companion.

Dawn was well underway by the time they got to their destination. They'd come upon the house with no warning, stepping out of the trees and onto an overgrown path fronting a large Tudor style manor house. At the sight of it, she'd stopped in surprise.

'Did you think I lived in a hovel?' Nate commented drily.

'I … well, no, but I confess, I wasn't expecting it to be quite so large.'

He laughed harshly. 'It might be large, but in truth, hovel is a good description.'

She looked over at him. 'Is it yours?' she asked carefully.

He gave a dark grin and nodded. 'Though I wish to God it wasn't.'

As they got closer, Mercy realised the house was in dire need of renovation. Even in the early morning half-light, she could see that the roof was sagging and some of the windows were boarded up. The area directly around the house had been cleared, but the rest of what had probably been formal gardens had been left to grow wild. The melting snow revealed glimpses of a carpet of wild bluebells.

She glanced over at him. 'Welcome to Carlingford Hall,' he murmured with a mocking bow.

She looked back at the mellow red brick wondering how it had come to be in such a sorry condition – clearly Nate Harding did not have the funds to do the necessary repairs. While she studied it, the sagging roof and missing windows became even more evident as the sun began to peep through the trees as it started above the horizon. It was beautiful, but sad.

'The stable's this way,' he growled, leading Duchess to the left and leaving Mercy to follow. As they walked, a sudden noise in the undergrowth preceded the arrival of his small dog. She'd been missing for the last half a mile and with the blood around her muzzle, it looked as though she'd been off catching her breakfast.

'What your dog's name?' she asked, running to catch up.

'Ruby,' he answered shortly.

'Have you had her long?' Mercy persisted, walking beside him.

'Since she was a pup.' His answer was brusque, and she realised he didn't want her questions. Too bad. If he'd not wanted her to know anything about him, he shouldn't have offered his help. Still, she subsided for now. Even if everything went according to their admittedly vague plan, it would likely be a couple of days before her father turned up. There was plenty of time, and she had to admit to being extremely curious about her gruff champion.

The stable appeared in much better repair than the house, giving another indication of the man's concern for the welfare of his animals. Indeed, it was another half an hour before he had the mare bedded down to his satisfaction while Mercy sat on the floor and watched. He hadn't suggested she went into the house without him, and she began to wonder just how bad it might be inside.

At length, he slung the panniers over his shoulder and picked up her bag before turning towards her with a muttered, 'Follow me.' Without answering, Mercy climbed wearily to her feet and followed him as he retraced their steps back to the front of the house. Rounding the corner, she saw the house clearly for the first time. Despite its shabby appearance, the house exuded a sense of peace, the like of which she'd never experienced before. Without thinking, she stopped and stared. Not realising she was no longer behind him, Nate continued on to the large front door, putting the bag down and pulling the key out of his pocket.

After pushing the door open, he finally turned, only to see she was still a distance away. Entirely mistaking the reason she'd stopped, he frowned. 'You have nothing to fear,' he stated flatly. 'You have my word that you will come to no harm in my house.'

Mercy blinked and started towards him. 'I know,' was all she said when she finally reached the door. For long seconds, they stared at each other, and Mercy's heart began thudding erratically. She abruptly realised that she no longer even noticed his scar. Indeed, her only thought at that moment was what would happen if he kissed her.

Chapter Seven

'What the hell do you mean she didn't get in the carriage?'

'I'm tellin' you she weren't there. The vicar and his missus got in, but she din't.'

Reinhardt swore. Had she somehow got wind of his plan? But how was that possible. He should never have talked to that damn priest. And his bloody arrogance in giving the pastor his real name could well come back to bite him.

'Search these premises. I don't care what excuse you use, just do it. If she's hiding anywhere in this building, I expect you to find her. How long ago did the carriage leave?'

'About ten minutes ago milord.'

'And the others are already in place?'

His companion nodded. 'All but me and Smiffy.'

'Send Smith to give them a message. They should remain where they are, but they are to let the carriage pass without interference if I'm not there. They are to do *nothing* – is that clear?' Another nod.

Dismissing his companion, Reinhardt gritted his teeth. There was too much at stake to give up at the first hurdle. There was no way the chit could have learned about his intentions. He'd spoken to no one except his cohorts and the priest. Feverishly, he thought back to his actions over the last couple of days, and his mind flitted back to the conversation in the stable last evening. Frowning, he thought back, going over the short meeting in the minutest detail.

He'd believed the stable empty but recalled the restless stamping of one of the horses. He'd ignored it at the time, thinking the horse's agitation was due to their unexpected presence. But what if there had been someone else there? Someone hiding behind the beast?

They would have heard everything.

Reinhardt swore again and aimed a frustrated kick at the chamber pot sitting next to the bed. The pot smashed against the door scattering pieces across the bedchamber. Fortunately, the pot had been empty. The knowledge that he could have spread piss all over the floor stopped him in his tracks. He needed to get a bloody grip. Letting his temper get the better of him wouldn't do.

He went over to the small desk and poured himself a brandy from the bottle he'd had brought up the evening before. Swallowing it in one fiery mouthful, he felt immediately calmer. Pouring himself another, he sat down in the armchair. If someone had indeed overheard his conversation with Davy in the stable, then the cat was out of the bag and there was nothing he could do about that. Clearly, the carriage was on its way to Cottesmore, which meant its occupants believed their charge to be safe. Had they put her in another coach? Sending her to her father by a different route? Reinhardt narrowed his eyes, taking a sip of his brandy. Not alone certainly. He needed to question the stable hands as to whether any other carriages had left the inn either late last night or early this morning and if so, who they belonged to.

The priest would undoubtedly be desperate to inform Stanhope of what had transpired. Murdering all the occupants of the carriage would certainly prevent that, but unless he tortured the information out of them first, he wouldn't discover the chit's whereabouts. Not to mention the fact that trying to force the information out of them would likely take far too long. By the time they confessed, Mercedes Stanhope would have arrived back in the bosom of her loving father and if he was caught, he'd almost certainly hang.

At the moment, he doubted they had any proof of his intention other than an overheard conversation. It would take them the best part of the day to reach Cottesmore and the Earl, which meant he had the rest of the day to track the bitch down. If he failed to abduct the chit, it was a setback, nothing more.

Reinhardt finished his brandy and stood up. Christian Stanhope might be aware he was coming, but the bastard couldn't be on his guard twenty-four hours a day, and ultimately, it would simply make the outcome that much sweeter.

***

After stepping through the door, Mercy instinctively paused to wait until her eyes adjusted. The inside of the house was dark and smelled overwhelmingly of mildew. As the entrance hall became clearer, she saw it was large and square with an imposing staircase rising up into the shadows.

Abruptly realising her rescuer had continued on down the hall, she picked up her skirts and hurried after him.

She passed two doors on the left, both firmly closed, and resisted the urge to stop and peek - especially when her would-be defender suddenly vanished. Fighting a sudden panic, she increased her pace and came upon a narrow corridor not visible from the hall. She couldn't help breathing a sigh of relief as she saw him waiting for her halfway down, outside another door. As she entered the narrow passageway, he pushed open the door, flooding the dank corridor with sudden light.

Seconds later, she followed him into a large, cavernous and very empty kitchen. Stopping involuntarily, she gazed about her. To the left was what looked to be a larder and to the right some kind of laundry room. The only pieces of furniture was a large table that had clearly seen better days, surrounded by three rickety chairs.

'How long have you lived here alone, Mr. Harding?' Mercy couldn't help asking. 'With the size of the kitchen, this house must once have been lived in by a large family.' She waved a hand around the vast space.

'It's a long story that has no bearing on the current situation,' was his short answer. 'And it's Nate.'

Mercy frowned. Clearly, he was telling her to mind her own business, but while she was under his roof and his protection, she felt she deserved to know more about her self-proclaimed protector.

Without asking, she seated herself at the table, taking care on the chair lest she ended up on the floor. 'I believe we have plenty of time on our hands … *Nate*. Clearly, you don't spend much of your time cleaning.'

'You don't know anything about me,' he bit out, putting the panniers onto the table and her bag at her feet.

'I am very well aware of my precarious position,' she answered, equally curtly. 'Which is why I am asking you questions. I am not requesting your life story, Mr. Hard... Nate. I simply wish to know a little more about you to put my mind at ease...' She paused before adding, 'And to reassure my father of your good intentions once he gets here.'

Nate's eyes narrowed as he stared at her. She stared right back. After a few seconds, he muttered something under his breath and began to remove the food he'd purchased from the two panniers. Pulling out a loaf of bread and a block of cheese, he fumbled in his pocket and brought out a pocketknife. Mercy's heart suddenly constricted at the sight of him unfolding the blade.

Using the knife, he hacked off a lump of bread and a piece of cheese, handing both to her. 'Eat, you must be hungry.' Mercy frowned, realising the kitchen did not contain either a fire or a stove. Nothing to cook on at all. Hesitantly, she took the bread and cheese off him, abruptly realising she was ravenous.

Making an effort to chew slowly, since she thought it likely that once the bread and cheese were finished, there would be nothing else, Mercy waited for him to speak. His absorption in his own food spoke volumes. As she waited, Ruby laid her head in her lap. Evidently, the terrier wasn't averse to a nonmeat diet.

'I've lived here since my father left it to me nearly ten years ago.' Nate declared abruptly. 'Since then, the house has been crumbling around my ears – exactly as he intended.'

'There was no money for renovation?' Mercy asked, intrigued, despite her avowal not to ask for his life story.

'Not a farthing,' Nate answered glibly. 'The bastard spent every last penny on the tables right up until the moment he drank himself to death.' He didn't apologise for his language, and in truth, being part of such a large family, Mercedes had heard much worse.

'It sounds as though he was a very unhappy man,' Mercy commented carefully.

Nate shrugged. 'He couldn't avoid leaving me the house and title, but he made sure the coffers were completely empty.'

'You have a title?' Mercy couldn't keep the incredulity out of her voice. Her companion gave a harsh laugh.

'Hard to believe, isn't it.' He gave a short mocking bow. 'Viscount

Carlingford at your service, my lady.'

Mercy frowned. 'But why did he not wish to leave you anything if you were his son?'

'As I said, it's a long and boring story,' he returned, clearly putting an end to the conversation. 'If you've eaten your fill, I suggest you get some rest. I suspect it's going to be a long two days for you.' He indicated the bread and cheese left on the table. 'While the weather remains as it is, the fare is not going to improve, I'm afraid.'

Resisting the urge to ask when he'd last eaten a hot meal, Mercy, broke her last piece of cheese in half and popping one half into her mouth, she handed the other to Ruby, who gulped it down happily. Then rising to her feet, she brushed off her skirt and waved him to precede her.

By eight a.m., she was ensconced fully clothed in a bed that looked and felt as though it had last been slept in during the Wars of the Roses. After a couple of experimental bounces, she felt as though she might never close her eyes again. Seconds later, she was asleep.

**

Reverend Shackleford was a worried man. And on this occasion, chatting with the Almighty really wasn't coming up to snuff. Signs and portents were all very well, but sometimes he needed a human audience. In truth, one particular human. He needed Percy.

They had passed the supposed kidnapping spot nearly an hour ago, and thankfully, nothing untoward had happened. Were they being followed? If Harding had not been feeding them faradiddles, then it seemed likely.

They'd left the inn an hour before that, with their three footmen protectors as well as the two coach drivers carefully surveying their surroundings, pistols in hand. Everyone had breathed a sigh of relief when they'd come into the next village after Corsham. Hopefully, it meant they'd successfully foiled Reinhardt's plot.

The Reverend wished his curate was here something fierce. As a confidante, Agnes was about as much use as Flossy. She'd spent the whole of the journey so far, gripping her salts and sniffing into her handkerchief, while Flossy snored in the corner. Somehow, Percy's presence gave added clarity to his thinking. He always came up with his best ideas when passing them by Percy first. Not that he needed the curate to actually *do* anything. Indeed, for the most part, Percy had about as much backbone as a dish of syllabub, but it had to be said his oldest friend was a deuced good listener.

In truth, Augustus Shackleford was dreading having to tell the Earl of Cottesmore that he'd mislaid his daughter. The fact that it had been Mercy herself who'd decided to abscond with a perfect stranger in the middle of the night was not going to hold water, no matter which way he looked at it.

He'd spent the better part of the last hour thinking of ways he could make the story a little more palatable, but so far, he'd come up with precisely nothing. And then of course, there was the added worry that Mercy *had actually absconded with a perfect stranger in the middle of the night*. Was she safe? What the devil would Stanhope do when he finally tracked Mercy down. Would he call Harding out? Force him to marry the chit? Had that been the scoundrel's plan all along? Had the whole kidnap story been a complete Canterbury tale?

The Reverend's thoughts were in danger of running away with him – indeed he'd actually been contemplating throwing himself out of the carriage - until he remembered his own conversation with Reinhardt and his conviction from the start that the fellow was involved in some havey cavey business.

No, whatever Harding was, he was honourable. The Reverend would stake his life on it. In truth, he might have to once the Earl got hold of him...

Chapter Eight

On waking, Mercy had felt horribly grimy but had been unable to do anything about it since the bedchamber didn't contain a washing bowl. Neither was there a mirror. In fact, the bed was the only piece of furniture in the room. There was, however, an old chamber pot situated under the bed for which she was particularly grateful, though she was uncomfortable at the thought of emptying it. She doubted the house contained a proper water closet, but wondered if there might be a privy of sorts. But then, given the age of the pot, she thought it unlikely.

In the end, once she'd seen to her needs, she'd pushed the pot back under the bed, straightened her hair using her fingers, brushed down her dress and finally stepped out into the shadowy hall.

She stood listening for a few seconds but could hear nothing - in fact, the silence was so absolute, it was unnerving. Suddenly disorientated, she walked slowly down the corridor towards a light which she hoped indicated the stairs. There were no pictures of any kind, and the wallcovering was so faded, she was unable to make out either the colour or the pattern.

After a few moments, she came to the top of the stairs and stared downwards, an unexpected sadness engulfing her. Clearly, the entrance hall had once been light and airy, but now the windows either side of the imposing front door were so grimy it was impossible to see anything through them. The chandelier hanging from the ominously sagging ceiling was cracked and coated in dust. Mercy shook her head as she picked her way carefully down the stairs. While she understood that Nate Harding hadn't got sixpence to scratch with, she was nevertheless surprised at the total lack of even the most basic repairs. The house was literally falling down around his ears, and he appeared to be doing nothing at all to stop it.

And yet the stable was in excellent repair.

On reaching the bottom, she hesitated. Should she retrace their steps from yesterday? There was still no sound of anyone else in the building, and if Ruby at least had been in the vicinity, Mercy had no doubt the dog would have heard her by now.

As she stood, Mercy abruptly became aware of the enormity of what she'd done. She was in a ramshackle old house with a complete stranger she knew absolutely nothing about – apart from the fact that he apparently had a title – which looking around her now, seemed more like a Banbury story.

Had she entirely overreacted? Spur of the moment actions were not Mercedes at all. Blunt, matter of fact, not given to wit and whimsy. That's how she'd be described by all who knew her. And yet she'd put herself in the hands of someone who could well turn out to be a madman – because of a story *he'd* told her.

She clenched her hands in sudden fear. Should she just collect her things and leave? Indecision engulfed her. She'd gone as far as taking a step back towards the stairs, when suddenly, the door to her left opened. Gasping in fright, she picked up her skirts to flee, just as the subject of her thoughts stepped through the door. He stopped on seeing her and they stared silently at each other.

'I made up the fire,' he growled, indicating behind him. 'The chimney's relatively clean, so it shouldn't smoke too much.'

Mercy looked past him into the room he'd just vacated. Aside from a cheerful fire burning in the hearth, the only furniture she could see were two winged chairs either side of the fireplace.

'It's not much, but it's more comfortable than the kitchen,' he added gruffly as the silence lengthened. Mercy's gaze came back from the room to focus on him. After a moment, she nodded without moving. He seemed to understand her hesitation and his lips twisted as he stated, 'You were planning to run.'

He hadn't phrased it as a question, but his stance indicated he wouldn't make any attempt to stop her.

Taking a deep breath, she shook her head and stepped towards the door. 'I was merely wondering which way I should go.' Walking past him into the room, she stared around her in surprise. It was a small sitting room, and unlike everything she'd seen of the house so far, this room was in good repair. The walls had been whitewashed and the floor polished to a high shine. It was possible to actually see through the window, and thick brocade curtains hung either side. While the two fireside chairs were clearly old, the leather had been carefully repaired and the cushions restuffed.

Glancing back, Mercy realised he hadn't moved, but was standing watching her. 'You spend a lot of time in this room,' was all she could think of to say.

He shrugged. 'Make yourself comfortable, I'll fetch you some tea. At her look of surprise, he gave a sudden grin which totally transformed his face. 'I'm not a complete philistine.' Mercy didn't answer - *couldn't* answer. She was completely transfixed by the unexpected difference in his features. Dear God, he must have been handsome before the scar.

Before she managed to find a reply, he was gone, shutting the door softly behind him. Mercy's heart thudded erratically. She didn't feel at all like herself as she sat down on one of the chairs. Her whole body tingled. What the deuce was wrong with her?

She twisted her hands in her lap, trying to focus her mind

on the problem at hand. She would be here no more than another day at the most. Her pocket watch told her it was early afternoon. Provided no more snow had fallen while she'd slept, her grandparents would be well on the way to Cottesmore by now, and once her father had been informed, she knew he would move heaven and earth to find her. Indeed, he might even arrive in the early hours. Unexpectedly, she was assailed by an absurd disappointment that this might be her only day here.

Mercy gritted her teeth. Carlingford Hall was entirely devoid of any comforts for pity's sake. Why on earth would she want to spend any more time in such a place? Nibbling on her fingernails, she tried to examine her feelings. She realised that for some absurd reason, she felt connected to Nathaniel Harding. Why, she couldn't even begin to say. His face was enough to provoke nightmares in any sensitive child, and perhaps because of that, he appeared to care for nothing and no one aside from his two four-legged companions.

But if what he'd told them last eve was true, he'd saved her from a fate worse than death. He could simply have left her to her fate, but instead, he'd warned her and offered his help. And despite her earlier fear that he'd made the whole story up, she didn't really believe that.

Her reverie was interrupted as the door reopened, this time, to admit Ruby who ran over in delighted abandon, rolling immediately on her back at Mercy's feet.

Laughing, Mercy bent down to stroke the wiry fur on the dog's belly.

'She has no finesse, I'm afraid.' At Nate's deep tones, Mercy's head snapped up. In his hands, he carried a small tray with a dish of tea and a plate of … something – she couldn't quite see what from this angle. She remembered the lack of cooking facilities in the kitchen and wondered how the devil he'd managed to make tea. He placed the tray down on the top of the mantel and handed her a dish. 'Be careful, it's hot,' he warned.

She frowned, taking the tea out of his hands and laying it on her lap, warming her fingers around the dish. 'How did you manage to make the tea? I don't remember seeing a fireplace in the kitchen.'

'It's in the scullery,' he answered, handing her a thick slice of bread liberally spread with honey. 'Don't ask me why.'

Suddenly ravenous, she took the bread off him and took a large bite, relishing the sweetness as it hit the back of her throat. She watched him take another slice for himself, then to her surprise, he sat down in the chair opposite. For one bizarre second, she felt as though they were an old married couple. As he sat down, Ruby immediately abandoned her, and went to sit at her master's feet, gazing up at him adoringly.

'It's not me she wants, it's the food,' he commented drily, breaking off a bit of bread and handing it to the terrier.

They were silent for a few moments until, at length, Nate leaned forward. 'Your father…' he began. Her heart slammed inside her chest at the thought of what he might be about to say.

'What about him?' she asked evenly.

Nate closed his eyes for a second, clearly thinking carefully about his next words. In the end, he sighed and simply said, 'We are in the same house. Alone. Will he insist on me doing the honourable thing?'

Mercy coloured up. She had known this conversation would have to be had. 'I think not,' she responded, putting the remnants of her tea on the floor for Ruby to finish off. 'May I be blunt?'

'Feel free.' Nate's response was wry.

Mercy took a deep breath. 'Perhaps he would have done if you were a good marriage prospect. In truth, I think he will believe you exactly the opposite.'

'Ouch,' Nate drawled, sitting back. 'And he would be absolutely right, of course. So, what do you think he will do?'

'I will of course assure him I have not been...' she hesitated, trying to find the right word...

'Molested, abused, ravished, ill-treated?' he suggested helpfully. 'I'm certain any or all will do.'

'Just so,' she sighed, picking at her skirt. 'It's my belief he will wish to keep the whole matter under wraps, so to speak. Though what he will do about the man who thought to abduct me, I cannot fathom...' She paused and frowned. 'My father does not forget, and I doubt he will rest until the blackguard is found, though in truth, I would prefer to forget the whole matter.'

'But what if he comes for you again?' Nate quizzed. 'Above all, I'm certain your father will wish to ensure your safety, and to do that, he must see that Reinhardt is apprehended.'

'Oh, I doubt the varmint will try again. I believe he was simply taking advantage of the moment.' Mercy's tone of voice was doubtful, despite her words of conviction. Nate knew she was trying to convince herself.' She twisted her fingers in her lap. 'I will, of course, insist you are suitably recompensed for your trouble.'

Nate regarded her, his face impassive. For a second, her heart galloped as she wondered if she'd offended him. She had no idea what he was thinking. Then abruptly, he shrugged. 'As you can see, I'm hardly in a position to refuse charity.'

'It will not be charity,' Mercedes protested vehemently, too vehemently perhaps. 'I could well be dead or worse if it hadn't been for you.'

He raised his eyebrows at her passionate defence of him. 'The saga is not done yet. We have to hope that your companions reach the Earl safely, but even in the fastest carriage, that will not be until sunset. Is it likely that your father will act immediately? Will he believe the priest's version of events?'

'The Reverend is my step-grandfather, so yes, I think he will...' She paused and couldn't suppress a grin at his look of disbelief. 'My father married his daughter, Chastity.'

'An earl wedding a vicar's daughter. You have an interesting family.'

This time Mercy laughed out loud, much to his bemusement. 'Oh, you have no idea,' she chuckled, shaking her head.

Nate stared at her. It was the first time he'd seen her smile, and when she did, she was simply breathtaking. To his complete disbelief, he felt an unwelcome stirring. 'You have an unusual name,' he observed, his voice gruff as he tried to get his cock under control. 'Was your mother Spanish?'

Mercy sobered and nodded. 'I never knew her. She died when I was young.' She offered no further information, saying instead, 'I believe my father will not wait until morning before searching for me.'

'Well, I doubt he will find it too difficult to uncover your whereabouts. I'm known in these parts, and...' He paused and gave a shrug, 'I have a face most people remember.'

'How did you get such a dreadful wound?' Mercy blurted the question she'd been wanting to ask since she first laid eyes on him. Then she winced and bit her lip. 'I'm sorry, that was terribly rude of me.'

Nate gave a humourless grin, his fingers reflexively touching the scar on his cheek. 'In truth, I'm surprised it's taken you this long to ask,' he commented ruefully after a second. She stared at him, and the compassion in her eyes nearly undid him. He didn't want her pity, God damn it.

'I took a bayonet wound in France, he answered curtly. 'It was a long time ago.' His tone made it clear he would say nothing more and after a second, Mercy nodded.

'So, should we expect your father before sunrise?' he commented instead.

Mercy frowned, then shrugged. 'Before noon certainly.'

'Would you care to make a wager on it?' he quipped, giving the same smile that had so captivated her earlier.

She cocked her head to one side. 'Do you gamble often?'

Nate chuckled, not at all put out by her question. 'I have nothing to play with. As I told you earlier, the only thing I own is this house, and I'm sure you'll agree that it's hardly a desirable wager, and besides...' He paused, then shrugged. 'I care not where I end up, but I would not see my only two friends on the street.' He waved towards Ruby, currently curled up next to the fire.

'So, I will wager the only thing I possess other than these four walls,' he continued flippantly, before rummaging around in the pocket of his breeches. Seconds later he pulled out a small box and opened it with a flourish. 'The one and only trinket I ever purchased.'

From her seat, Mercy could see it was a small ring. Her gaze flew to his, but his expression gave nothing away. She bit her lip, wondering who he'd bought it for and why. Without taking her eyes from his, she touched the large gold locket lying in the hollow of her throat. 'This came from my mother, so I will not risk it on a gamble.' She thought for a second, then held up a hand to slide a ring off her finger. 'This is my wager,' she declared, holding the band out.

'That is not an even stake,' he murmured hoarsely, staring at the ruby studded ring. 'I think it is,' she answered simply. 'I think they were both purchased with the same sentiment.'

69

Nate gave a bark of laughter and shook his head. 'I doubt it,' he chuckled, snapping the small box shut and tossing it onto the floor between them. 'The person I bought it for many, many moons ago, took one disdainful look before declaring in no uncertain terms that she wouldn't even get out of bed for a stone smaller than a pigeon's head.'

***

Reinhardt had no choice but to begin packing. Despite extensive enquiries, no one had seen the chit leave. And the only other carriage hadn't departed until early afternoon. He was beginning to regret not questioning the priest, but still believed the risks had far outweighed any potential rewards.

He gritted his teeth in frustration. Why the hell hadn't he stuck with his original plan? Acting rashly never paid off – he of all people should have known that. Now, he'd alerted Stanhope not only to his presence in England, but to his intentions. What would have been a simple snatch had he waited until the chit was in London was now going to be so much more difficult.

But the discovery that Mercedes would be travelling alone but for two elderly chaperones had seemed too good an opportunity to miss. And when his informant in Cottesmore had learned that accommodation in the Black Swan had been arranged, Reinhardt had believed the abduction would be easy. Especially when he discovered there was even a damn preacher staying at the same inn. He could have wedded and bedded the bitch before Stanhope had known anything about it. Instead, he'd made a complete mull of the whole thing. Starting with his impulsive conversation with the bloody priest who'd turned out to be one of the elderly chaperones his source had mentioned.

Reinhardt threw the last of his clothes into his bag. He knew Stanhope would come for him and he needed to be long gone before the Earl got here. He'd revert back to his original plan to snatch her in London during the season.

Unless of course Stanhope decided not to attend.

Reinhardt swore savagely and fought the urge to throw something. His hands clenched and unclenched as his rage threatened to get the better of him. He didn't dare lose control now. He couldn't fail. If he did, he'd lose everything. He took a deep shuddering breath as the anger finally began to dissipate. Stanhope wouldn't cancel what was likely his daughter's final chance at making a good match. She was three seasons in and well on the way to being a permanent fixture in his house. His younger wife would almost certainly want to be rid of a tiresome stepdaughter.

No, Mercedes would have her season - Stanhope was arrogant enough to believe he could protect her. But no matter how vigilant, her father couldn't watch her every minute of every day, and that was exactly when he'd strike. By the time Stanhope got his head out of his arse, the two of them would be halfway across the Atlantic and well on the way to securing her mother's legacy. But for now, he needed to lay low. As soon as the priest mentioned his name, Stanhope would wait only until he was assured of his brat's safety before coming after the man he believed had murdered his child's mother.

Chapter Nine

'Start at the beginning if you please, Augustus. And explain to me slowly and carefully exactly why my daughter is not in the carriage with you.' While the Earl's voice was entirely devoid of emotion, there was a small tick in his right jaw that did not bode well at all. Indeed, the Reverend very much feared that underneath the icy exterior, his son-in-law was visualising him roasting slowly over hot coals.

Swallowing, Augustus Shackleford started the story from the moment they left Tewkesbury. As soon as he mentioned the name of the American man he suspected was behind the kidnapping attempt, Christian lost all semblance of calm. 'You're sure that was the man's name?' he shot back savagely.

The Reverend nodded. 'He even told me how to spell it.' Abruptly, the Earl swore softly then groaned, his face ashen.

'Do you know this man, Christian?' Chastity asked, unable to hide the fear in her voice at the sight of her husband's look of horror. He nodded and climbed back to his feet.

'I take it you won't say no to a brandy, Augustus?' He didn't wait for a response but went straight to the decanter on the sideboard.

'Could you pour one for Agnes and me?' Chastity added to his back after a quick glance towards the wilting matron.

After handing everyone a glass, the Earl pulled the servants' bell before picking up his own brandy and knocking it back in one fiery gulp. Then pouring himself another, he returned to his chair. As he sat down, there was a knock at the door, and seconds later, the housekeeper entered. She took one look at the sober faces around the room and shut the door behind her.

'Mrs. Scott, would you ask Joseph to ready the carriage with fresh horses and bring it round to the front within the hour? Have him rouse John and Thomas with my apologies if they are already abed. Unfortunately, I will need their services again.

'Has something happened, my lord?

Christian sighed. 'Mercedes is missing,' he answered shortly, ignoring her small gasp and holding his hand out to forestall further questions. 'I'm afraid I know very little more than that at this point in time, Mrs. Scott, but your help – and your discretion - would be very much appreciated.'

The housekeeper nodded, giving a quick bend of her head. 'I'll speak with Joseph immediately, my lord.'

As she went back through the door, Christian turned back to the Reverend. 'Pray continue, Augustus. Once you've told me everything, I will give you the bare facts about Oliver Reinhardt.'

It took another fifteen minutes for Reverend Shackleford to provide the full story as he knew it. 'Perhaps I was wrong not to accept this Harding's assistance in the first place,' he finished. 'Mercy certainly thought so – that's why she took matters into her own hands.' He indicated the note, now lying innocuously on the table.

Gripping her husband's hand, Chastity shook her head. 'Much as it surprises me to be saying this, I really don't think you can blame yourself, Father. You did what you thought was best.' She looked over at Christian who nodded reluctantly.

'Mercy may be pragmatic, but she's also headstrong when she gets a notion into her head.' He grimaced. 'Tossing blame around benefits nobody. What matters now is to get Mercedes back. You are sure this Harding will not harm her? You do not believe him to be in league with Reinhardt?'

'I believe him to be an honourable man,' the Reverend answered vehemently. 'He will keep her safe.'

'And he had a dog,' Agnes added unexpectedly. 'Pretty little thing and well looked after. Flossy took to them both.' She shrugged as though such canine approval was more than enough reason to trust the man. Perhaps it was. Christian relaxed visibly. Appropriately, the subject of her conversation chose that moment to emit a loud snore from her place by the fire.

'Now then, about this deuced blackguard, Reinhardt?' The Reverend stared at the Earl expectantly.

'He was – is I suppose - a professional gambler from Boston. He's a vicious bastard with the morals of an alley cat. He's also insane.' He paused and rubbed at his brow before adding, 'and I have reason to believe he killed Mercy's mother.'

Chastity gasped in shock, and Christian took her hand, raising it to his lips. 'Forgive me, my love. I never spoke to you about him as I never imagined for one second that he'd follow me across the Atlantic. In truth, I thought him dead - it's been fourteen years since I last laid eyes on him. He took a deep breath and shook his head. 'We haven't the time now, but I swear that once I return with Mercy, I will tell you everything I know about him.'

'You can enlighten me in the carriage,' the Reverend interjected bluntly.

'Absolutely not, Augustus. I must insist you stay here. You've already had an arduous journey, and forgive me for saying it, but you're no spring chicken.'

The clergyman gave a rude snort. 'Poppycock. And anyway, you need me since I'm the only one who can recognise Reinhardt as he is now.'

'I doubt he's changed that much, and the fact that you arrived here in one piece likely means he was aware Mercy wasn't in the carriage and assuming he hasn't managed to track her down – and I'm praying to God he hasn't – then I'd expect him to be long gone. He knows I'll come for him.'

'Well, he's come a deuced long way and gone to a lot of trouble to steal her from under your nose, so I doubt very much he'll give up quite so easily. I don't believe we've seen the last of him.'

Christian gritted his teeth, then nodded with a sigh. 'I fear you're right.' For a second, he felt weighed down with despair. There was so much he hadn't yet revealed, but he wanted to speak with Chastity alone before sharing the information with her father and very likely others. Nicholas Sinclair would need to be informed, at the very least. He looked over at his wife and was heartened by the trust in her eyes. She knew there was much more to the story than he was revealing but trusted him to tell her when the time was right.

'I will get Mrs. Biddle to prepare you both a small repast,' she declared climbing to her feet. 'Then I'll go up to the children. I would prefer them not to know that their sister is missing.' She smiled at Christian as he stood up and took her into his arms.

'Thank you,' he murmured hoarsely.

'I will hold you to account when you return,' she returned firmly. 'Please do not even think to whitewash this tale, Kit. I am not some delicate flower to be protected.'

'Well, given that you actually climbed a tree into my bedroom in order to speak with me on only our second meeting, I think you use the word delicate far too loosely.' His voice was dry as he bent to kiss her.

'Don't try and fudge it Christian Stanhope,' she ordered, leaning back to look up at him. 'I will expect a full accounting.' She laid the palm of her hand on the side of his face, softening her words. 'Bring her home to us.' Then, biting her lip to prevent sudden tears, Chastity made her way to the door before abruptly stopping and turning round.

'I know you will not allow Christian to leave you behind, Father, but please don't do anything foolish.' She turned to Agnes. 'I'll have Mrs. Scott bring us both a tray of supper, Stepmother. I'll be back down as soon as I can.'

'Thunder an' turf, I wouldn't want to be in your shoes when you get back,' muttered the Reverend as the door closed decisively behind her.

***

To the Reverend's frustration, the Earl refused to divulge any further information about Oliver Reinhardt during their return journey to the Black Swan, and since the clergyman was in truth done to a cow's thumb, he soon fell asleep, propped up in the corner of the carriage, Flossy snuggled under his cassock.

Although Christian had sighed in exasperated aggrievement at his father-in-law's insistence in bringing the little dog along, the Reverend had dug in his heels, maintaining that Flossy had always provided invaluable assistance in the past and he had no reason to suppose she wouldn't be of use now. Especially if they needed help tracing where Harding had taken Mercy. 'She's got the best nose I've ever known since Freddy, God rest his soul,' was his excuse.

Fortunately, by the time they got on the road, the snow had already begun to thaw and they made excellent time, arriving at the inn just after dawn. After ordering them both some breakfast, the Earl immediately began asking questions.

The Reverend was remembered from the day before and one of the first things the innkeeper told them was that another man had been asking about his party after they'd left. 'Shifty lookin' cull, 'e was. Weren't from these parts – 'e 'ad a funny way o' speakin.' He caught the Reverend's look of anxiety and added, 'Don't you worry none, Revren, I'm as much in the bloody dark as you are, but even if I 'ad seen summat, I wouldn't 'ave told no bloody furrener anythin'.'

'Do you know if any of your workers happened to see someone leave in the early hours of yesterday morning?'

'I don't reckon, though Jed – 'e works in the stable – said there was an 'orse missin' when he went in. He din't realise the 'orse wos gone at first since the bloke insisted on lookin' after the beast 'imself.'

'May we speak with him?' Christian asked, hope stirring.

'I'll tell the missus to fetch 'im.' The innkeeper hurried away, leaving the two men to their breakfast.

'It has to be Harding,' the Reverend deduced. 'He said he'd overheard Reinhardt's conversation while he was in the stable.'

'Do you know why Harding was staying here if he lives only a couple of miles down the road?'

'His horse had taken a stone to her shoe and the inn was closer, so he said.'

''Ere 'e is, Milord.' The innkeeper had returned with a small man in tow.

'I din't see 'im leave, yer lordship, an' yest'day we wos that busy, I din't notice the 'orse wos gone until nigh on sunset since the cove had insisted on lookin' after the animal 'imself. Asked fer a poultice an' some stew as I remember. Ugly fella 'e wos – the bloke, not the 'orse...' He paused to chuckle at his own joke, but seeing their serious faces, gave a small cough and hurriedly continued. 'Wore a scarf round 'is face nearly all the time, but I saw 'im pull it down fer a few seconds and 'e 'ad a scar right down the side of 'is face.'

'Do you know who he was?' the Earl asked urgently.

'I'd never seen 'im before, but when I told Dilly about it last night – it wos me night off an' me an' Dilly are courtin – she reckoned it sounded like the fella wot lives in Carlinfud 'all.' He gave another pause and fiddled with his cap before adding, 'You know what, Milord, all this talkin' 'as me throat right parched...' and looking at the Earl expectantly.

Sighing, Christian ordered a tankard of ale be brought to their table. 'Pray continue,' he demanded in a tone no one in their right mind would argue with.

The ostler gave a small bow. 'Thank you kindly yer lordship, that's right kind of you.' He caught sight of the Earl's narrowed eyes, and hurriedly got back to his tale. 'As I wos sayin. This fella, he lives in a big old 'ouse about two miles from 'ere. Keeps 'imself to 'imself on account of 'is 'orrible scar. I reckon 'e must 'ave took a sword to 'is face durin' the war.

'Did you tell any of this to the man who was asking questions yesterday?' the Earl quizzed him.

Jed shook his head. 'Don't 'old wi' furreners, 'an anyway, I din't remember 'til I told Dilly yest'day evenin'.'

'So, his house is called ... Carlingford ... Hall? And you say it's a couple of miles from here?'

The small man nodded. 'As the crow flies, I'd say. If you wos takin' a carriage, you'd 'ave to go all the way to the crossroads, then turn left. The track to the 'ouse is about a mile down that road. I'll warn you though, you'll not get a carriage the size o' yours down there easy, an' I don't reckon the fella wot lives there is over fond o' visitors.'

Christian nodded his thanks and handed the ostler a shilling. 'Thank you, Milord, this'll go towards our weddin'. Dilly's right keen to tie the knot as soon as possible.' Christian fought a smile at the young man's glum face. Clearly, Jed wasn't in quite such a hurry to get leg shackled.

***

Nate was still sitting at the kitchen table as the sun came up, though he took no note of the glorious artist's palette of orange and gold splashed across the sky. All he could see in his mind's eye was Mercedes Stanhope's face.

And he knew without doubt that allowing her into his life was the biggest mistake he'd ever made in the whole of his sorry existence. He should have found some other way of helping her. *Anything but bring her here, into this house.*

He put his head down into his hands in anguish. How could he have known that simply seeing her sitting across from him, conversing with her would make him *want*.

After the long-ago humiliation with Genevieve, he'd been so bloody careful. Kept himself to himself - focused entirely on his army career. Being so far away from England had suited him perfectly. And then came Waterloo and he didn't have to guard his heart anymore. Who the hell would want someone who looked like a monster out of some dark fable?

His reaction to Mercy had taken him completely by surprise. He'd thought himself immune to a pretty face, but it wasn't just her face, lovely as it was – it was everything about her. And in the deepest corner of his heart where he kept the dreams he barely even acknowledged to himself - she was exactly as he imagined his wife would look.

A low whine had him lifting his head up to see Ruby staring at him anxiously. He shook his head to clear it. What the bloody hell was he doing to himself? Climbing restlessly to his feet, he told himself that his reaction was simply because she was the first female with whom he'd shared an actual conversation since … in truth he couldn't remember when. He whistled for Ruby and headed towards the door. Mercedes would be gone by the end of the day and out of his life forever. Dreaming about things that could never be, was not how he'd made it this far. Focusing on the here and now, putting one foot in front of the other – that was how he'd survived the loneliness.

The problem was, he'd opened Pandora's box and glimpsed the one thing he wanted more than anything else, and now he had no idea how to shut it again.

Thrusting the treacherous thoughts out of his head, he stepped outside and breathed in the crisp, cold air, directing his footsteps round to the front of the house. But before he had the chance to step off the path towards the distant trees, Ruby began barking. Seconds later, a carriage appeared round the bend in the drive.

Chapter Ten

Mercedes was awake long before dawn. Indeed, she'd spent the majority of the night tossing and turning, her mind going over and over the events of the day before, starting with their ridiculous wager.

Nate had bet that her father wouldn't arrive until after ten in the morning, while she declared categorically that he'd be here before eight. And just like that, they'd gone from being complete strangers to ... she wasn't sure what exactly.

Though he'd said no more about who he'd bought the ring for, she learned that he'd received his scar during the Battle of Waterloo and that the man who inflicted it had been trying to remove his head at the time.

'I was one of the Duke's aides-de-camp and on my way to give him a message. Fortunately, his grace saw me fall and had me taken to his own surgeon. The man saved my life.'

'Were you riding Duchess?' Mercy asked, shuddering at the thought of what the battle must have been like for both horse and rider.

He nodded. 'She took a wound to her side. The only reason she wasn't destroyed on the spot was because I refused to leave her. Neither of us fought again after that day.'

'Where did you go?'

For a moment, Mercedes thought he wouldn't answer, then he sighed. 'I was recuperating for months – couldn't even get to Brussels. And when I was finally well enough...' He shrugged. 'I had nothing to come home for.' He gave a dark chuckle and waved his hand around the room. 'My triumphant return to the ancestral pile only took place once my father was dead and buried.'

She wanted to ask him why he'd lived like a hermit from that day. Clearly, the scars he carried were not solely physical. Instead, he firmly steered the conversation back to her and she found herself telling him all about her family.

When he went to check on Duchess, it seemed the most natural thing in the world to go with him, and standing in the stable, feeding the mare a wizened carrot while Nate looked at her hoof, she felt a surprising sense of peace.

Dinner, Nate informed her was courtesy of Ruby who on this particular occasion had been quicker than the rabbit she'd been chasing. It didn't happen often apparently.

And the oddest thing? She was in a house in the middle of nowhere, completely alone with a man she'd met only hours ago, but at no time did she feel even the remotest fear. It was the strangest day Mercy had ever spent, but truly, she hadn't wanted it to end.

As soon as the light started to fail, he'd bidden her a courteous good night and she'd retired to her bedchamber to find a bowl of washing water, a small sliver of soap and a freshly washed chamber pot...

And now, lying in the sagging, worn bed, she finally acknowledged to herself that she didn't want to leave Carlingford or Nathaniel Harding. She squeezed her eyes shut, allowing the bewildering feelings and emotions to have their way with her. She realised it was madness. She hardly knew him – and from the small amount she'd discovered, it was abundantly clear he was a man with many demons. But, for the first time in her life, she *wanted* to learn more.

Would her father allow him to visit her at Cottesmore? Would he even want to? And to what end?

Her thoughts continued to gallop through her head, one after another as the crack between the moth-eaten curtains gradually became lighter and lighter. Dawn couldn't be far off. She guessed Nate would already be up and about. How long would they have before her father arrived?

Her musings were abruptly interrupted by the sudden cacophony of barking outside. Ruby, clearly. Climbing out of bed, she hurried to the window and peered through the curtains, just in time to see a carriage coming up the drive.

The answer to her last question was no time at all.

***

Nate ordered Ruby to sit as he watched the carriage make its stately way towards him. His stomach churned. Whatever ridiculous dreams he'd harboured through the night finally withered entirely. He would be lucky to survive the next hour.

Despite his sudden urge to make himself scarce, Nate forced himself to step forward when the carriage finally drew to a stop. As the door opened, to his shock, a small bundle of fur came hurtling out and headed straight for him. It was the little dog who'd been with them at the inn. She capered around his ankles, and as he bent down to fuss her, the sense of doom hanging over him began to dissipate. When she turned her attention to an excited Ruby, he straightened and watched as Mercedes' step-grandfather climbed down.

'I hope for your sake you've kept her safe, Harding,' the Reverend grunted as he turned to look back at the carriage. Before Nate had a chance to answer, the last occupant appeared at the door, and he got his first look at Mercedes' father. Despite his inner turmoil, Nate's face was impassive as he watched the Earl jump agilely down the steps.

'Do you have anywhere the horses can rest and get some water?' the Earl enquired politely.

'There's a stable towards the back of the house.' Nate pointed out the direction to the coach driver. 'My horse is in there but there should be plenty of room for another four. There's fresh water in the trough and a sack of oats.'

While Joseph unhitched the horses with the help of two footmen, the Earl turned back to Nate and regarded him coolly.

'Your daughter is safe and unharmed, my lord,' Nate offered guardedly after a second.

'Then I am in your debt, Mr. Harding.' Despite the courteous words, Nate didn't miss the Earl's undertone of relief.

'I believe she is still abed. Would you care for refreshments while you wait for her to rise?'

Christian nodded. 'That would be most welcome, thank you.'

'Lead on, Harding,' the Reverend interjected loudly, waving towards the front door. 'I hope you've got a half decent bottle of brandy stashed away in this pile somewhere.'

Somewhere, Nate thought, resisting the sudden unwelcome urge to laugh. He had no idea where he'd left the bottle he'd been determinedly working his way through – was it only four nights ago? He led the way to the front door, hoping he didn't have to shove too hard to get the damn thing open. Fortunately, he'd had the foresight to keep the fire burning in the sitting room, so despite the tomblike coldness of the rest of the house, the small room at least would be cosy and cheerful.

Nate winced as the two men followed him into the hall. He knew the Earl would be taking everything in, despite his aloof exterior. Mercy's grandfather wasn't quite so polite, muttering, 'Thunder an' turf, lad, I think you need to do a spot of redecorating. I can see daylight through that deuced crack.' Fighting the urge to tell the blunt clergyman to mind his own bloody business, Nate gritted his teeth and opened the sitting room door.

'If you'd like to make yourself comfortable, my lord, I'll bring you both a glass of brandy. Would you like some tea with it?' The Earl nodded with a rueful glance towards his father-in-law who was already making himself comfortable in one of the armchairs.

Directing his parting comment to the elderly cleric, Nate endeavoured to keep his voice civil. 'Whilst you are perfectly correct in your assessment that the house needs some work, you'll be relieved to know that I don't believe any part of it is likely to fall on your head during the short time you're in it.' With that, he stepped through the door and shut it firmly behind him, only to see Mercy standing at the bottom of the stairs.

They stared at each other silently for a second. 'Your father's arrived,' Nate said needlessly at length. She was hardly likely to have missed his arrival since the carriage had stopped right under her bedchamber window. 'I trust you slept well,' he added when she continued to stare at him mutely.

As she nodded finally and took a step forward, Nate felt a sudden insane urge to walk over, pull her into his arms and cover her mouth with his. The shocking intensity of the desire nearly brought him to his knees. Dear God, how long had it been since he'd kissed a woman? 'Would you like some tea?' he said huskily instead, wondering if he'd lost his mind.

'That would be lovely,' she answered, her voice soft and uncertain. Had she picked up on his desperate need? His cock was straining against his breeches, a fact she couldn't have failed to notice had she dropped her eyes from his face.

Feeling like some kind of depraved madman, Nate swallowed, willing the evidence of his desire to go down. 'Your father and grandfather are in the sitting room,' he said gruffly, when he could stand it no longer. 'I'll fetch some tea.' Then he turned and fled.

*

'As you can see, I'm perfectly well, Papa. Mr. Harding has been kindness itself.' The Earl stepped back from their embrace and looked down at his daughter. An unexpected lump formed in his throat at the thought of what could have happened to her.

'He didn't … take advantage of you in any way?' Christian probed, staring down at her searchingly.

Mercy gave an emphatic shake of her head. 'Without his help, I could very well have been in this Reinhardt's clutches by now. I trust you will see him recompensed, Father?' Christian didn't miss her switch from her childish Papa to a more formal address, and he sighed, realising she truly was no longer his little girl. He nodded.

'Naturally.' He paused and looked round the room before adding a rueful, 'God knows, he could do with it.'

'Who is this man who thought to abduct me, Father? I mean, I know his name, if that's his real one, but why me?' Christian winced. He'd hoped this conversation would wait until they were back at Cottesmore. He watched Mercy seat herself in the other chair, gathering his thoughts.

'As for who he is – all I can tell you is that he's an inveterate gambler hailing originally from Boston…' he paused choosing his next words carefully. 'I believe he knew your mother.'

Mercy had been turned towards the fire, holding her hands out for warmth. At his words, her head shot up. 'They were friends?'

The Earl shook his head. 'I don't believe there was ever a friendship between them...' Another pause. How the devil could he tell his daughter that her mother was a courtesan and Reinhardt had likely been one of her clients?

To his relief, he was saved from answering as the door was pushed open, to reveal Nate, balancing a large tray with one hand. Moving over to help, Christian was glad to see Harding had unearthed a bottle of passable brandy. He didn't usually imbibe so early in the day, but he couldn't deny that after the pressures of the last few hours, a tot would be very welcome.

As the only two seats in the room were already taken, Christian and Nate stood awkwardly in front of the fire. For a few seconds, silence reigned as they sipped their tea until the Earl finally placed his dish on the mantlepiece and picked up the brandy.

'I think this will likely be more beneficial at the moment,' he murmured drily. After staring down into its amber depths for a moment, he gave a sigh and turned to Mercy's rescuer. 'I owe you a debt I can never repay, Harding, but I trust you will allow me to go some small way to repaying it by having the essential repairs done to your house.' He watched Nate colour up, and for a second, he thought pride would make him refuse the boon.

But after a moment, the man grimaced and shrugged. 'I would be a fool to turn down such an offer. Thank you, my lord. As you're clearly aware, the repairs are long overdue.'

'Bit of an understatement, I'd say lad. The deuced place'll be falling down around your ears by the end of next winter.' As usual the Reverend didn't mince his words. 'Are you in Dun territory, or just purse-pinched?'

'None of your damn business,' Nate growled before he could stop himself.

Reverend Shackleford didn't take the least offence. 'So, it's purse-pinched then. I take it you were left the property but no blunt to upkeep it.' He shook his head sadly.

'Mr. Harding has a title,' Mercy interrupted – erroneously in truth, since the title clearly hadn't put food on the table or filled the holes in a leaking roof. Nevertheless, both her father and grandfather looked surprised.

Nate winced, then bent his head with a sigh. 'Viscount Carlingford at your service, my lord,' he offered wryly.

The Earl frowned. 'I thought the name Carlingford sounded familiar. You're Gerald Harding's son? I'd thought him lost at sea.'

Nate gritted his teeth. He really didn't need this conversation right now. 'You're correct, my lord. My esteemed older brother did indeed end up in a watery grave. I am the second son.'

Christian raised his eyebrows. 'Forgive me, I wasn't aware that Harding had had any more children. I was under the impression the title had lapsed.'

Nate spread his hands and shrugged. 'As you can see, my lord, it didn't.' He gave a humourless laugh before adding drily, 'What can I say, I was always more my mother's son – literally.'

Christian stared at him for a second, then nodded his head in understanding. So, it wasn't simply grief that had led Gerald Harding to drink himself to death. The knowledge that his title would pass to another man's bastard must have been galling to say the least.

'Have you not thought about taking your place in society?' he quizzed, thinking it best to change the subject.

Nate stared at him impassively for a second. 'Aside from the fact that I haven't got sixpence to scratch with, as the good Reverend described so succinctly, my face is not exactly my fortune.'

'It's none of my business,' Christian countered evenly, 'but there are many who would pay handsomely to obtain a title for their daughter. A pretty face is not mandatory.'

There was a small silence until at length, Nate responded flatly, 'As you say, my lord, it is no one's business but my own.'

Christian sighed, knowing he'd pushed the man too far. 'I think we have presumed upon your hospitality for long enough,' he said brusquely, finishing his brandy. 'My man will call on you over the next few days to assess which repairs are the most urgent. I trust I do not have to tell you that what happened here must not go beyond these four walls?'

Nate bowed his head. 'You have my word. If...' There was a pause as the Earl looked at him enquiringly. The Viscount glanced over at Mercy who was looking at him, her face inscrutable. He took a deep breath. 'I do not believe you have seen the last of this Reinhardt, my lord. Should you require my assistance in safeguarding Lady Mercedes at any time in the future, I offer it gladly.'

It was on the tip of Christian's tongue to declare that he took care of his own, but given the events of the last three days, he swallowed the blunt reply and instead, inclined his head in return before adding a brisk, 'Duly noted,' before turning towards Mercedes. 'I think it's time we went home, love.'

'Thank you for the brandy, Harding,' the Reverend commented, climbing laboriously to his feet. 'It was more than passable, and your house might be a draughty old pile, with more holes than roof, but I confess, I've seldom sat in a more comfortable chair. Had I stayed there much longer, you'd have had to carry me out.' He looked down at Flossy, curled up next to her new friend. 'Come along, Floss, time to go.'

Mercy's heart was already thudding unsteadily as she got to her feet. Nathanial Harding's comment about helping to keep her safe had given her the beginnings of an idea, but she knew it needed much more thought before she brought it out into the open. As her father and grandfather made their way to the door, she faced the man who had taken her into his protection and likely saved her life.

'I cannot thank you enough for your generosity, my lord,' she murmured, keeping her eyes on his chest as her face unaccountably coloured up. 'Without your intervention, I don't know what would have happened.' She gave a small curtsy, before finally lifting her eyes to his where she fought a gasp at the brief flare of emotion in their depths. She had time to realise that his eyes were beautiful, the colour of warm dark honey, before the shutters came down.

'The honour was mine,' he answered huskily, bowing his head in return.

For a fleeting second, they stared at each other, then Nate deliberately took a step back and waved his hand towards the door, murmuring a hoarse, 'After you, my lady...?'

Chapter Eleven

Augustus Shackleford was unusually quiet during the journey back to Cottesmore. Despite Chastity's declaration that what happened had not been his fault, he couldn't help feeling responsible. If he'd have taken up Harding's offer of sanctuary, Mercedes would not have been put in a such a precarious position. If anyone found out that she'd spent the better part of two nights alone with a man ... well, a good match was the last thing she'd make.

And what if the blackguard Reinhardt did show his face again? If he did, it would no doubt be in London. Her father couldn't provide Mercy with bodyguards everywhere she went – that would cause a scandal in itself. Neither could the Earl be on hand every time she stepped outside the door. Mayhap he would have her forego the season, but if he took such a step, he would very likely be condemning his daughter to lifelong spinsterhood.

And Mercedes Stanhope deserved to be mistress of her own home with a man who would cherish and take care of her. The Reverend gave himself a mental shake. He knew he was being fanciful. *Ton* marriages seldom came with such considerations – in truth, his daughters had all been uncommonly lucky. But nevertheless, she deserved to have what might be her last opportunity.

Reverend Shackleford came to a decision. *He* would accompany her to London. No one would question a man of the cloth, especially when that man was her grandfather. And whilst they were there, he'd deuced well find out where Reinhardt was holed up and put an end to the varmint.

For that he'd need the help of his son-in-law, Jamie Fitzroy. The Reverend knew that since Jamie had become a magistrate, he and Prudence spent the majority of their time in London. It wouldn't take much to convince both of them to help – especially as Pru would likely be in if she fell in...

But there was one more person vital to the success of a such a mission.

He needed Percy.

It had been far too long since the two of them had done a spot of sleuthing together. Reverend Shackleford oft felt guilty that the responsibilities of the parish had by and large been taken over by his curate. Naturally, his guilt did not extend to taking them back, but nevertheless, the Reverend felt it was time for Percy to put his responsibilities aside for a time and have a little excitement.

Of course, the possibility that searching the streets of London for a madman with a penchant for kidnapping young ladies might actually be his curate's worst nightmare, simply never occurred to him...

***

As he read Augustus Shackeford's missive, Percy Noon felt as if a large hand was tightening gigantic fingers around his heart. The Reverend's strongly worded *request* to accompany him to London had taken the curate back to their last disastrous visit to the Capital - although, in all fairness, it hadn't been quite so disastrous for King George, since their interference in his coronation had actually prevented the monarch's assassination – but nevertheless, Percy still found himself waking up in a cold sweat from nightmares in which he'd been trying to force himself through endless crowds surrounding Westminster Hall in time to prevent the King's murder.

And now, of course, there was Finn. Even if he found someone to take over the parish services, how could he leave Lizzy to deal with Finn on her own? The lad was busy finding his feet, and as his self-confidence grew, so did his proclivity for mischief. Without a father's hand, Percy very much feared the boy would run rings around his mother.

Putting the letter down, the curate put his head in his hands. He couldn't simply ignore his superior's entreaty, and what was worse - if he was being entirely honest with himself, there was even the tiniest hint of anticipation at the thought of once again being embroiled in some havey cavey business.

The Reverend had not written what the *havey cavey* business actually was, but Percy knew it was something to do with Mercedes. An explanation would be forthcoming once they were in London. Fortunately, that wasn't going to be for another couple of weeks, so at least Percy would have the chance to prepare Lizzy and locate a temporary replacement – or in the Reverend's words, 'Find someone in the village who can read, and hand him a Bible.'

Some things never changed...

***

'I thought you hadn't known much about Mercedes' mother,' Chastity said carefully when they were finally in the privacy of their bedchamber. She was folding her clothes away, having dismissed her personal maid early.

This was the first opportunity they'd had to discuss Reinhardt. In the initial euphoria of having Mercy back, both Christian and Chastity had deliberately kept the conversation away from the subject of her near abduction – predominantly because they didn't want the twins to be alarmed.

Although the Reverend had maintained his Friday face throughout most of the meal in protest at being kept in the dark, Mercy herself had seemed more than content to leave any serious discussions until the morrow.

To Chastity's surprise, her stepdaughter had seemed less than enthused about her safe return to Cottesmore and was quiet and withdrawn throughout dinner. At first, Chastity had thought her traumatised, but as the evening went on, she didn't think that was the case. It was more as if Mercy was deep in thought - and having seven sisters who'd sported similar faces when contemplating tying their garter in public, Chastity was understandably filled with some disquiet.

Fortunately, Agnes had inadvertently kept the younger ones entertained with a lurid description of the time a seagull dropped a winkle in her ear, so Chastity's careful observation of her stepdaughter went largely unnoticed. Except by her husband of course. Indeed, Christian had expected Mercy's preoccupation to be the first thing they talked about after retiring, but like most women, Chastity had surprised him by her opening gambit.

Sighing, he sat down on the edge of the bed. 'In the letter she left, Mercy's mother declared she had consumption. I couldn't simply abandon her to her fate. At the very least, I owed it to my daughter to ensure her mother was taken care of.' He looked down at his hands. 'I hired a private detective to investigate her whereabouts. That private detective was Oliver Reinhardt.'

Chastity frowned, sitting beside him. 'I thought you said he was a gambler?'

'He was, though I didn't know it at the time. He was recommended to me by an acquaintance – one who apparently owed Reinhardt a lot of money. The bastard didn't confine his games to the tables. I found out later that he was acquainted with Mercy's mother. Had even possibly been one of her clients. He'd known where she was from the onset, though he led me a merry dance with his *supposed* investigation.' Christian paused, passing his hand wearily over his face. Clearly the memory was distressing. Chastity said nothing, allowing him to speak.

'She was being taken care of by a Catholic mission. By the time I got to her, she was very close to death and far too frail to be moved. Reinhardt had been playing me for weeks while Mercedes lay slowly dying in a cold cell. I've never felt so helpless. All I could do was give the nuns enough coin to ensure she was as comfortable as possible. I visited her daily. I sat there, staring at the face of a woman I hardly knew but who'd actually borne me a child...' Chastity gripped his hands as she spied tears gathering in the corner of his eyes.

'I told her how I would look after our daughter. Described in detail the life she would have. I didn't really believe she could hear me, but then, one day, she gripped my jacket and pulled me closer to her, trying to tell me something.'

'What was it?' Chastity asked, intrigued despite herself.

Christian sighed again. 'I never found out. By then she was just drifting in and out of consciousness, drenching the sheets with blood during every coughing fit. I left, and when I returned the next day, she'd gone. I identified the body and had her interred in a grave with a proper headstone. It felt like far too little too late.'

Chastity leaned towards him and gently kissed him on the mouth. 'You did what you could,' she murmured. 'If she'd come to you earlier, I'm certain you would have helped her.' She touched his face. 'What happened with Reinhardt?'

The Earl grimaced. 'He came for his money. It was only afterwards one of the nuns told me he'd been visiting her for weeks – long before I turned up. They seemed to think she may have had something of his.

'And then I was told he'd been with her when she died. Apparently, she'd drowned in her own blood as he'd tried to force some information out of her – what, I have no idea.' He shook his head, and clenched his fists, turning to face Chastity and saying harshly. 'I left the mission, went to find Reinhardt, and beat him within an inch of his life.

'Not long after that, I booked passage for England.' He stopped and sighed before adding. 'I have never heard his name mentioned since I left him broken in an alley... Until yesterday.'

'Why do you think he was looking to abduct Mercy? Could it have been revenge?' Chastity asked.

Christian shook his head. 'I thought about his motives during the carriage journey this morning. That he hates me I've no doubt. But right from the onset, he seemed a singularly cold individual. He might be enjoying the thought of exacting revenge, but it's not his primary motivation – just an added bonus.

'No, there's another reason he wants Mercy, and I can't help but think it has something to do with her mother.'

'Did you discover anything else about her? Could she have come from a wealthy family perchance? I mean, with what you've told me of Reinhardt, it seems likely that his interest would have been purely mercenary.'

Christian grimaced. 'It may have been remiss of me, but I didn't seek to find out whether she had any family. I didn't wish to risk there being another claim on Mercy. She was my daughter, and that's all there was to it.'

Chastity smiled and leaned forward to kiss him. 'You've been a wonderful father to all our children.'

Her husband gave a rueful grin. 'I can just about cope with four.' He leaned forward to deepen the kiss, but she pulled back.

'What do you intend to do about Reinhardt? I can't imagine you'll simply leave him to his devices. If he does have some nefarious scheme in play, he's unlikely to stop at one try.'

Christian nodded. 'The more I think about it, the more certain I am that we've not seen or heard the last of him.' He paused, then added, 'I'm not sure I should allow Mercy this season. But if I don't...' he left the rest unsaid, and Chastity sighed in understanding.

'I'll speak with her, of course, but I'm of a mind to contact Nick and Adam for their reaction. Whatever happens, I cannot simply leave Reinhardt to his own devices. Somehow, we have to draw him out into the open.'

Chastity felt her heart constrict at his words. 'We can't put Mercy at risk, Kit.'

He shook his head and lifted his hand to touch her cheek. 'You know I wouldn't do anything to put any of you in danger, my love. I'll find a way to catch the bastard without risking everything I hold dear.' He bent forward to kiss her, but again Chastity pulled back, leaving him regarding her with raised eyebrows.

'Did you notice that Mercy seemed very preoccupied at dinner?'

To her surprise, he laughed. 'There's the question I was waiting for.'

Chastity frowned, 'Was I that obvious?'

'Only to me darling. I noticed too. Perhaps she's simply anxious.'

Chastity shook her head. 'No, that wasn't the look she had on her face. It was the look of someone planning something.'

'And naturally, that's an expression you're very familiar with,' he returned drily. His wife nodded and frowned.

'This Viscount Carlingford – was he very disfigured?'

Christian thought for a second. 'Well, he wouldn't go unnoticed at a ball, let's put it that way.'

'But is it possible that a young, sheltered woman might be taken with him?'

Her husband regarded her steadily. 'Are you asking me if she's formed an attachment to Harding?'

'Well, has she?'

'There was no evidence of it,' he answered carefully, 'though being a man, I'm oblivious to such nuances. He's certainly no oil painting now, but I believe he might have been considered handsome before his injury.'

Chastity frowned again. 'You say his pockets are to let?'

'Hasn't a feather to fly with.'

'Do you think he's a good match for Mercy?'

'What, despite the fact that he hasn't got the blunt to do even the most basic repairs to his property and has a face that's likely to give small children nightmares, you mean?'

She narrowed her eyes at him and nodded.

Christian opened his mouth to speak, then shut it again, his brow creased in thought. 'I think our Viscount has a lot of demons,' he responded at length. 'From what he told me, I believe he was the result of an affair his mother had whilst married to his father - and I think said *father* never let him forget it.

'As far as I can tell, when his eldest son and heir died, Gerald Harding set about spending every penny he had – mostly on alcohol and gambling if I remember rightly. He left nothing but an almost derelict house and a title.' He paused and shook his head before adding, 'I'd thought the title had lapsed to be honest.'

'Did he tell you how he got his hideous scar?' The Earl shook his head.

'Apparently, he told Mercy he received it at Waterloo.'

'Ah, so he was confiding in her then.' Chastity narrowed her eyes.

'I cannot think that meant anything. Clearly, they had to talk about *something*.'

Chastity sat in silence for a moment, pulling at the ribbon tying back her hair. 'So, if we put aside possible Banbury stories, do you think Mercy's dowry would be sufficient to cover both the repairs to the house and allow him to keep her in relative comfort?' Chastity asked bluntly.

Christian shook his head at her with affectionate exasperation. 'I think you're forgetting one thing, my love...' He paused as his wife regarded him quizzically. 'We have no actual idea whether Viscount Carlingford actually wishes to get leg shackled...'

Chapter Twelve

By the following morning, Mercy had come up with a workable plan. Of course, like any plan, it depended very much on the people executing it, and since her plan involved Viscount Carlingford pretending an attachment to her in order to provide an escort while she was in London, well … in truth, it was still a work in progress.

Would he even consider being party to a fake engagement in order to keep her safe?

Certainly, his presence would provide her with the additional protection she needed whilst ensuring she could peruse the current crop of young men on offer without feeling as if she was a prize heifer taken to market. It would also go a considerable way to providing the penniless Viscount funds needed to continue with the repairs to Carlingford.

Which led her back to her original question – would he do it? After all, he'd spent over fifteen years hiding away from the world - mostly because of his awful scar. But, while his face might well provoke considerable speculation, Mercy was persuaded that most women would see past it to the honourable man underneath. So, not only would she benefit, but there was every possibility that he would find himself a rich wife. '*Like me*,' a small voice whispered in her ear.

Naturally, she ignored such a preposterous idea.

She dressed carefully for breakfast, having been told by Felicity Mackenzie - the Duchess of Blackmore's oldest friend and mentor to all of them – that one should always regard clothing as a weapon to be wielded with careful precision. Today she needed to appear older than her years – both sober and sensible.

Muttering the words like a mantra, she made her way downstairs to the breakfast room where her three half siblings were already enjoying their breakfast.

'Has somebody died?' Kate asked, eying her admittedly sombre attire. Mercy looked down at herself with a slight grimace. Had she done it a little too brown?

'No one's kicked the bucket,' Ollie scoffed. 'If they had, Mama would be wearing black and she has her green dress on today.'

'You shouldn't say *kick the bucket*,' Kate retorted. 'Papa will put you over his knee.'

'Grandpapa says it all the time - and he's a vicar, so God must have told him it's not rude.'

'He says Tare an' hounds too,' Kit piped up and Mama says we shouldn't say it because it has to do with…' he paused and looked around before whispering, '*Gambling.*'

'What's gambling?' Kate asked.

'You're too young to know about such things,' Kit declared loftily, earning him a kick under the table. 'Ouch,' he yelled.

Mercedes sighed, seating herself at the table. 'Where are Mama and Papa?' she asked, taking a piece of toast.

'Papa's in his study. He said to tell you and Grandpapa to meet him there once you've finished breakfast.

'Tare an' hounds, I feel like I've been run over by a deuced coach and four.' As their grandfather stomped in, Kit threw a smug look at his sisters earning him another kick.

'You've travelled a long way, Grandfather, I'm not surprised you're a little out of sorts,' Mercy sympathised with a warning glare at her three arguing siblings. 'How is Grandmother feeling this morning?'

'She's taken to her bed,' the Reverend muttered, helping himself to some bacon. 'When I last saw her, she was eating a soft-boiled egg. If we're fortunate, she won't get up before Tuesday,'

'Do you think she'd like me to visit, Grandpapa?' Kit asked solemnly. 'I could read to her.'

'I'm certain she'd be delighted,' the clergyman responded with a small chuckle.

'We'll come with you, won't we Ollie?' Kate declared, pushing her chair away from the table.

Seconds later, they were gone. 'That wasn't very charitable of you, Grandfather,' Mercy reprimanded him when her siblings were out of earshot.

Reverend Shackleford sighed and crossed himself. 'You're undoubtedly right, my girl, but I don't believe even the Almighty would begrudge me a little amusement in return for putting up with Agnes for more than a quarter of a century. In truth, I'm fortunate to still be here the number of times the woman's tried to poison me.'

'Oh, I'm sure that's not true,' protested Mercy vehemently before adding, 'not intentionally, anyway.'

'So, tell me about this fellow Harding, then, the Reverend demanded, changing the subject as he tucked into his bacon. 'I take it he didn't get up to any mischief?'

'Grandfather!' Mercedes gasped. 'I can assure you, the Viscount was at all times the perfect gentleman.'

'Oh, *the Viscount,*' is it now?' Reverend Shackleford looked up and raised his eyebrows.

'I'm simply using his correct title.' Mercy gave a small, self-conscious cough and determinedly pushed back her chair. 'I'll take Flossy out to do her business whilst you finish your breakfast. Father wishes us to join him in his study.'

'Do you think he wishes to talk about *the Viscount,*' the Reverend quizzed to her back. Mercy stiffened her back as she heard him chortle. He might be a man of the cloth, but he could be such a child at times.

***

As Mercy sat and listened to her father's discourse on how he intended to manage her season without telling anyone or putting her at risk, she gave every indication that she was listening intently. Inside, however, she was simply biding her time until the opportunity arose for her to put forward her intricately devised plan. However, when the Earl finally paused for breath, and just as she was about to speak, her grandfather got in first.

'There's no cause for concern, my lord. It's all sorted, I've been in touch with Percy...'

'Already? Which part of, *I'd rather you didn't tell anyone,* didn't you comprehend, Augustus?'

The Reverend frowned, truly nonplussed. 'Well, it wasn't just anyone. It was Percy.'

Christian sighed and waved the clergyman to continue.

'We will accompany you and Mercedes to London,' the Reverend declared in the same tone he might have said, 'I'll give you the Crown Jewels.' He paused and stared at his son-in-law expectantly.

'Why?' To be fair, the Earl's response was relatively mild considering the sudden grip of panic that caused his stomach to roil most unpleasantly.

'Why, to chaperone Mercy, of course,' Reverend Shackleford retorted, wondering why the Earl looked as queer as Dick's hatband. 'I mean, who else is going to accompany her while she's purchasing fripperies or out for an afternoon stroll? We'll even accompany her to balls and whatnot. You'll have no cause for worry, lad. Percy and I will simply blend into the shadows. We'll...' He stopped, suddenly realising his audience were staring at him in what might have seemed like horror to a less sensitive individual. But then, it was rather dark in here. He gave a satisfied nod before adding, 'Naturally, Agnes will return to Blackmore.'

'Well, we can be thankful for that small mercy at least,' Christian muttered drily.

'I'm certain such a jaunt will be entirely too much for you, Grandpapa,' Mercy declared, her speech unaccountably shrill, 'though I'm exceedingly humbled that you would be so kind as to offer your services, of course.' She turned to her father, her voice taking on a desperate tone. 'It will be entirely too strenuous, don't you agree, Father?'

'Unquestionably,' the Earl commented between gritted teeth. The mere thought of having to keep an eye on his father-in-law as well as his daughter had him tempted to throw himself out of the window and be done with it.

The impervious clergyman waved their protests away, and Christian suddenly realised that the Reverend actually *wanted* to accompany them to London. He wasn't simply assuaging his guilt for allowing Mercy to run off on her own. Staring at his father-in-law's heroically sincere face, the Earl opened his mouth to declare he might as well have Mercy delivered to Reinhardt on a silver platter, when fortunately, or unfortunately, his wife chose that moment to enter the room.

'Am I interrupting something?' she asked into the deafening silence.

'Grandfather was offering to continue his services as a chaperone, but I told him it would be far too much for him,' Mercy told her in a tone that left Chastity in no doubt as to her daughter's opinion on the matter.

'I'll have Percy,' the Reverend reminded her with a beatific smile. Naturally, the clergyman had omitted the part where he and Percy intended to root out Reinhardt and bring the blackguard to justice...

'Well, in truth, I can't see that it would do any harm,' Chastity responded. Ignoring her husband's and stepdaughter's glares, she took a seat. 'If Mercedes is to have her season, as I see it, the more people surrounding her, the better. You won't be able to accompany her wherever she goes, darling, and if Father is willing...'

'I have a proposal,' Mercy declared loudly in nothing like the reasonable tone she'd practised in front of the mirror earlier. As three sets of eyes looked at her enquiringly. She took a deep breath and explained...

***

Nate silently watched the Earl's man taking notes while shaking his head at the state of the ceiling and looking pointedly at the bucket placed strategically on the floor. Without speaking, the man then started up the stairs, testing every tread with his foot. An ominous creaking sound accompanied more than one step, and Nate had to fight the urge to show the smug little toad out using the end of his foot.

Instead, the Viscount gritted his teeth and followed, half hoping the man would disappear through a convenient hole in the staircase.

When the Earl's inspector had first arrived, Nate hadn't known what to think. He'd half believed Cottesmore would get to the end of the overgrown drive and wash his hands of the whole affair.

But to his surprise, the very next day, a Mr. Jamison had arrived, offering him the worst thing possible - hope.

Since she'd left the day before, and despite repeatedly telling himself, he was completely addled, Nate had been unable to get Mercedes Stanhope out of his mind. All the common sense in the world couldn't smother his desperate urge to see her again, and he found himself concocting all kinds of increasingly outlandish scenarios where he and Duchess would ride to her rescue, sweep her up in his arms, and... Well, that's where the fantasy got stuck. The most he could hope for was her friendship. But he told himself it was enough.

Just to see her again, talk to her and watch her animated face. That he was a fool, Nate had no doubt. A man didn't fall in love with a woman after only two days, even if she represented everything he'd ever wanted.

A timely reminder of who and what he was, came from the top of the stairs. 'Are you aware my lord, that you currently have a brace of pigeons nesting in your master bedchamber?'

No, he didn't bloody know that, since the last time he'd stepped foot in the master bedchamber had been the day he received the key.

Grimacing, Nate forced the treacherous thoughts out of his head and went to have a look.

**

As Mercy finally stuttered to a halt, her audience was ominously silent, until at length, her father commented evenly that he hadn't known she was possessed of such an imagination, or indeed inclined to such flights of fancy.

Her grandfather simply snorted and told her she was dicked in the nob to even consider enlisting the help of a man whose idea of etiquette was likely using a fork instead of his fingers. 'And besides, who the devil is going to believe it.'

'Since when has a pretty face been a prerequisite for an engagement?' Chastity commented thoughtfully, echoing her husband's earlier comments. 'We know that Viscount Carlingford is purse pinched, but since he's never appeared in public, no one else does. I'm certain the *ton* could be persuaded with very little effort that he is as rich as Croesus and has simply been reclusive due to his terrible injury heroically received during the Battle of Waterloo.'

'And how do you think Harding will take such a proposal,' Christian quizzed her. 'At the very least he will be making himself the subject of gossip.'

'That as may be, but he will also benefit. If his house is as bad as you say, he'll likely be without a roof over his head within the next couple of winters. This way, he has a chance to find a wealthy wife.'

'I thought we were spreading the rumour of his vast wealth,' her husband reminded her drily.

Chastity shrugged. 'At the end of the day, he has a title.'

'I think it's a huge assumption to suppose Harding actually wants any assistance in finding a wife. We know nothing about him except that before he overheard the supposed plot to abduct Mercy, he was living his life and minding his own business. Now you're looking to turn his life upside down. He'd be perfectly within his rights to accuse us of making a May game of him.'

Christian's voice was hard and after a moment, Chastity nodded. 'You're right. I'm speaking of him as though he's a child in need of guidance.'

Mercy bit her lip, knowing her father was right. It was all very well to decide that the Viscount could not help but benefit from his association with them, but he'd shunned the world of the *ton* for many years. Why on earth would he consider putting himself in a position where he would most likely be ridiculed at the very least? Of course, her father was overlooking one simple factor.

In her heart of hearts, Mercy knew Nathaniel Harding would do it for her. She thought back to his face as he'd stared at her outside the sitting room. He was hers for the taking - she knew it right down to her very toes.

But did she want him? Could she risk trampling all over his heart, only to discover that the connection she thought was there didn't exist back in the real world? And how would her father react if he knew what she was really thinking?

She became aware that her grandfather was speaking again. 'Well, much as it pains me to admit it, if the fellow fought at Waterloo, he'd likely be useful in a fight.'

'What about you, Mercedes?' It was a second before Mercy realised her father was speaking to her. She looked at him silently, trying hard to suppress an inevitable blush. 'Why are you so willing to put your life into a stranger's hands?'

How could she say that the Viscount intrigued her more than any other man she'd ever met? That she wanted the opportunity to get to know him better, and this was the only way she could think of to do it? It was a mutton-headed plan at best. And completely selfish.

She opened her mouth to tell him to discard her idea - that she was being extremely foolish - but what came out instead was, 'I trust him.' And it was true, she did – she hadn't hesitated to trust him with her life.

There was a silence, then Chastity sighed and gripped Mercy's hand while addressing her next words to her husband. 'All this conjecture is getting us nowhere. If you think the idea of enlisting Viscount Carlingford's help has any merit at all, perhaps we should simply go ahead and ask him. It's not as if he is unaware of the threat Reinhardt presents.'

The Earl steepled his hands, pondering her words. 'So, let's assume Carlingford agrees for a moment. For the *ton* to accept his ongoing presence as Mercy's escort, he would have to play the part of a devoted fiancé convincingly. And Reinhardt himself needs to believe it real. The dual purpose of the charade would be to keep Mercy safe and force Reinhardt into acting rashly, - hopefully revealing himself in the process.' He paused before directing his next words to Mercedes.

'Once the danger has passed, how do you propose to end your engagement to the Viscount? I seem to remember being told of your Aunt Patience playing a similarly dangerous game with Max during her come out. That whole smoky business had a happy ending, but I think it unlikely that history will repeat itself.' He shook his head doubtfully. 'I feel as though we may well be trying to use a sledgehammer to drive in a nail...'

Chapter Thirteen

Mercy was silent while her father wrote the note to Nathaniel Harding. Her thoughts were going round and round in her head – a ceaseless cacophony of questions she had no answers to. She'd had no idea how she would end her fictitious engagement and couldn't make her mind up as to whether she would even want to. And then there was the guilt about using a man who had already gone through so much in his life. She had never been so confused about anything in her entire life. And on top of all that was the fear that Reinhardt might succeed in his bid to force her into wedlock.

So far, her father had spoken very little about the American's reason for wishing to abduct her. He claimed Reinhardt was a gambler and a fortune hunter – and while she believed him to a point, Mercy was almost certain there was something he wasn't telling her. Something to do with her mother. Whether he was protecting her sensibilities or trying to lessen her fear, she wasn't sure, but for the moment she was content to let sleeping dogs lie. First things first – would the Viscount agree to help them.

To help *her*.

Mercy knew the request for aid from a stranger didn't sit well with her father, and she also knew he was sending two more letters – to the Duke of Blackmore and the Earl of Ravenstone. Both had become close friends over the years, and Mercedes was well aware that asking for aid from Nicholas and Adam was much more to her father's liking. That said, neither man was in a position to provide what was needed to draw Reinhardt out of hiding. And unfortunately, Mercy didn't have a surfeit of potential suitors prepared to put their lives at risk to protect her.

She told herself that Nathaniel Harding's lot would be hugely improved by their association. He would be able to complete the repairs to his house, and if he wished, take his place in society – even putting aside her confused emotions about the whole matter.

As her father handed the three missives to the messengers, she couldn't help wondering what Jennifer and Victoria would say if they knew what was happening. In truth, none of her other seasons had started quite so eventfully...

***

Nate stared down in consternation at the letter in his hand. Why the devil would the Earl of Cottesmore invite him to visit? Thrusting aside his sudden fierce elation at the thought of seeing Mercy again, he read through the missive a second time. Though couched in flowery language, Nate recognised it wasn't simply a social invitation. The Earl wanted something from him.

Laying the note on his lap, he absently stroked Ruby's head. To turn down the invitation would be unforgivably ill-mannered, and though the knowledge irked him, the fact of the matter was, he needed the Earl's favour. Especially after learning that the essential repairs to Carlingford were significantly more urgent than he'd previously believed.

The messenger hadn't waited for a response. Clearly, Christian Stanhope did not expect him to refuse the invitation. Nate looked down at the letter again. He was to present himself the day after tomorrow in time for dinner. Even riding Duchess, it would take the best part of a day to reach Cottesmore, so he'd have to leave at dawn. The Earl hadn't patronised him by offering to send a carriage.

Closing his eyes, Nate leaned his head back and wondered if he actually possessed any clothes suitable for dinner at an Earl's country estate. He presumed the invitation would extend to an overnight stay, so not only would he need evening attire, but a change of clothes for the following morning.

Hopefully, he'd be able to unearth something that was relatively clean, or at the very least stain free. He shook his head. The events of the last week had provided the most excitement he'd had for more than a decade, and sitting alone in his sitting room, Nate discovered something interesting about himself.

The Earl's invitation definitely had him intrigued, so perhaps that meant he hadn't entirely lost all enthusiasm for life. With a soft chuckle, Nate climbed to his feet and went searching for something to wear...

***

Reverend Shackleford frowned as he read Percy's letter. Was the curate actually suggesting he should bring Finn with him to London? Thunder an' turf, that would be a disaster. How the devil would he and Percy find the time to look into the whereabouts of Reinhardt if they were spending all their deuced time babysitting?

The Reverend had written to Prudence and Jamie to tell them he and Percy were going to be in London though he hadn't told them why, except to say they would be staying at Christian and Chastity's townhouse. Naturally, the clergyman had been hoping that if Harding agreed to pretend an attachment to Mercy, he and Percy would be free to do a little more snooping. There wouldn't be much chance of that if the curate was bacon brained enough to bring his son along.

Reverend Shackleford sighed. Investigating such smoky

business was all very well – after all, aside from his God-bothering duties as Dougal Galbraith referred to them, it was what he did best – but the Earl was right. He wasn't getting any younger. And as much as he was loath to admit it, the journey from Scotland had taken a lot out of him.

The Reverend was just about to pen a letter telling Percy that under no circumstances was he to allow Finn to accompany him to London, when the clergyman suddenly had another thought.

Finn was light-footed and quick. And whenever he stopped talking long enough to actually think, the lad had a sensible head on his shoulders. He was also small for his age and might well come in useful if they needed him to squeeze into a tight space for a spot of eavesdropping. At the end of the day, bringing the boy along might not be such a bad idea after all.

Naturally, they wouldn't actually put him in danger – there would be no sticking him up any chimneys for example – Lizzy would string them both up if they did, but there was no denying, having another pair of eyes that didn't need deuced eyeglasses to see beyond the end of their nose would be very useful indeed.

Augustus Shackleford nodded to himself in thoughtful satisfaction. It was all about thinking creatively, and if there was one thing the Almighty had gifted him with, it was an ability to come up with ideas that lesser men might consider a trifle bird witted.

Things were coming together nicely. Providing Harding agreed to play the loved-up suitor, he, Percy and Finn would be free to find Reinhardt and hopefully have him shipped back to the Americas before he managed to cause any more deuced trouble...

***

Mercedes stared at herself in the mirror, turning this way and that to see herself from every angle. This wasn't usual for her at all - any more than giving consideration to the colour of her dress, or how low the neckline should be. Usually, her tendency was to give whatever she was wearing a quick glance and, providing she was showing nothing untoward, she was content.

Tonight, however, she was wearing a dark apricot dress with large gigot sleeves which had recently become all the rage. Fitted across her bosom with the skirt flaring from her waist, it showed her curves to quite the advantage. Though in fairness, *curves* might be putting it a little strongly - but at least she had a reasonably small waist.

The warmth of the apricot suited her olive colouring too, and her hair, held back in a simple chignon, appeared almost mahogany in the early evening light, while her eyes had taken on the colour of melted chocolate.

All in all, Mercy was satisfied she looked her best. Forcing down a sudden bout of nerves, she offered her maid a warm smile of thanks and picked up her reticule.

She'd been aware the moment Viscount Carlingford arrived. The noise created by both Flossy and Ruby would have alerted the whole house to the fact, even had a footman not been watching out for him.

Rather than go down to greet him along with her father and stepmother, Mercy had remained in her bedchamber, biting her fingernails, all the while reprimanding herself for her cowardice. But since he'd arrived barely an hour before dinner, she told herself she had a perfectly valid excuse.

Now of course, she'd simply made matters worse. Gritting her teeth, she took a deep breath, stepped out of her room and headed towards the stairs.

As she got closer to the small drawing room, she could hear voices and wondered whether her father had already broached the subject of their possible fake engagement or was perhaps waiting for her arrival. Swallowing nervously, she lingered at the door for a moment before abruptly realising that her step grandfather was one of those already in the room. With a sudden fear of what might possibly come out of his mouth if left unchecked, she hurriedly pushed open the door and stepped inside.

All eyes turned towards her, and she faltered, her eyes immediately flying towards the Viscount who swiftly got to his feet. They stared at each other, everyone else in the room disappearing for a few heart-stopping moments. He looked very different from the last time she'd seen him, though his attire certainly looked to be somewhat out of date. As he bowed, she responded with a small curtsy before looking anxiously to her father.

'Well, you took your time girl,' the Reverend boomed. 'I was beginning to think we'd have to wait until tomorrow morning. But now you're here, perhaps we can get this whole deuced business settled so I can enjoy my dinner.'

Mercy swallowed a retort rebuking the Reverend for his rudeness, experience telling her it was simply water off a duck's back. Instead, she seated herself next to her stepmother who took her hand encouragingly.

Her father turned to the Viscount as the maid offered Mercy a glass of punch. 'Though his manners leave a little to be desired,' the Earl offered drily, 'my father-in-law is nevertheless correct, my lord. I believe we owe you an explanation for requesting your presence at such short notice. May I call you Nate?' At the Viscount's surprised blink, Christian gave a boyish grin. 'It's a tradition in our family, started I believe by the Duke of Blackmore who has no time for ceremonious poppycock as he refers to it.'

Nate shrugged and nodded his head. 'Certainly, I've been called much worse over the years.' He gave a tight grin.

'Well, Nate, perhaps I should start by properly introducing my family. This is my wife, Chastity, her father, Augustus, and of course, you've met our eldest daughter, Mercedes. We have three other children, all of whom you will likely meet at breakfast.'

The Viscount bent his head. 'Is your lady wife indisposed?' he asked the Reverend politely.

'Almost permanently,' the clergyman answered with a sigh.

'Agnes is prone to megrims,' Chastity interjected. 'Hopefully, you will have the opportunity to meet her before you leave,' She ignored her father's muttered, 'I wouldn't hold your breath,' and smiled warmly.

Christian picked up his glass of wine and took a sip, clearly thinking how to phrase his next words. 'I believe your quick-thinking kindness prevented my daughter's abduction from the Black Swan,' he said carefully at length. 'But what you are not aware of, is that this man was no simple opportunistic fortune hunter, but someone I know from my time in America.'

Nate raised his eyebrows but did not speak, allowing Christian to continue. 'His name is Oliver Reinhardt. He is a gambler and a liar.' The Earl then went on to describe everything he'd told his wife earlier, leaving nothing out. Since much of the tale was new to both Mercy and her grandfather, the room was silent until he'd finished.

'I don't know exactly what it is that Reinhardt wants of Mercedes,' Christian finished, taking care to address his last words to Mercy. 'But my gut tells me it's something to do with her mother.'

No one spoke for a few seconds as they digested the Earl's tale. The Reverend was the first to speak. 'So, you think this blackguard wants Mercy under his control for something more than curtain lectures?'

The Earl nodded, then spread his hands. 'Unfortunately, I don't know what.'

'You think she had something he wanted?' Mercy asked, fighting a sudden urge to cry. She could remember very little about her mother, but talking about her like this had turned her into someone real, and it was the first time the Earl had spoken at length about her death. She watched carefully as he nodded.

'I do. Though I can't imagine what it might be. I made limited enquiries into your mother's background, but other than that she came from Mexico, I unearthed nothing. My suspicion is that Reinhardt had known her for some time – perhaps back when she was in Boston. Mayhap she told him something about her family.'

'Do you think I still have relatives in Mexico?' Mercy asked in a small voice. Her father shook his head.

'That I cannot say. If we can apprehend Reinhardt, perhaps we can persuade him to tell us.'

'All this is very interesting,' the Viscount declared, 'but forgive me, my lord, I do not see what it has to do with me. Naturally, I am overjoyed that I was able to prevent Lady Mercy's abduction, and if you wish for my continued help, I give it willingly, though I never actually saw this Reinhardt so could not tell you what he looks like.'

'I sat across the table from the varmint, so once we get to London, we could easily commission a sketch.'

'London?' The distaste evident in the Viscount's voice spoke volumes, as did his accompanying frown. He looked round at the three expectant faces before adding carefully, 'I think perhaps now would be a good time to tell me what it is you wish of me.'

There was a short silence, then the Earl took a deep breath and told him...

Chapter Fourteen

Mercy never took her eyes off the Viscount's face throughout her father's clarification of how they hoped to lure Reinhardt out into the open. His expression remained carefully neutral, though she couldn't help noticing a tightening of his lips when her father spoke about the proposed fake engagement.

When the Earl finally finished, the only sound in the room was Flossy's and Ruby's snoring next to the fire.

'Pray tell me why anyone with eyes in their head could possibly believe that Lady Mercedes Stanhope would even consider a marriage proposal from someone who looks like me?' Nate's voice was harsh, and Mercy flinched. She wanted to tell him that his scar was inconsequential. That once one got to know him as a person, it became hardly noticeable. But he'd lived with the shame of his disfigurement for more than fifteen years, and she knew her platitudes would not be welcome. Nor would he believe her.

Instead, her stepmother leaned forward and repeated her earlier statement. '*Ton* alliances are not formed based on one's looks. You might have been out of society for many years, but I am certain you're fully aware of that my lord. You have a title, and if people believe you wealthy, your disfigurement really does become irrelevant.'

She took a deep breath, before continuing candidly, 'I believe we can trust you. You fought at Waterloo so you can clearly take care of yourself in a fight, and if necessary, we believe you can protect our daughter.

'But most importantly, you are an unknown. Your betrothal to Mercy will be the talk of the season. The gossip it will generate will be sure to get to Reinhardt's ears, and, we *hope*, propel him into acting hastily…' She paused before adding, 'I know we are asking an awful lot of you based solely on the compassion you have shown to Mercedes thus far, but it is my hope that you will also benefit.'

'Ah, so you're offering to pay me, my lady.' Nate gave a humourless laugh. 'And what do you suppose my price will be?'

His flippant question was answered by her husband. 'I will ensure your house is entirely in order and help you generate an income from the land surrounding it. My influence and that of my brothers-in-law will ensure you are accepted by society and able to take your place within it should you so desire. If in time, you wish to take a wife, you will have something worthwhile to give her.' The Earl's tone was even.

Nate nodded slowly, before turning towards Mercy. 'How do you feel about the gossips calling you a fool behind your back?' he quizzed.

'I care not what people call me,' Mercedes scoffed. 'But I am entirely certain that once you are known, the gossips will change their tune.'

'And when the time comes, how will we end our *engagement*?' he asked. 'Naturally, I do not wish people to pity me any more than they do already.'

'Once Reinhardt is caught, it's my intention to disclose the whole charade,' Christian stated firmly. The other four stared at him in astonishment. This was a surprise to everyone.

'There will be no chance of Mercy being compromised since it's my hope that she will be well chaperoned to every function you both attend.' He gave a low chuckle before adding, 'This family has any number of females who'll be more than willing to throw themselves into the charade.'

'Have you been in touch with Nicholas?' the Reverend asked.

'Naturally,' Christian responded. 'And Adam. My hope is that both Grace and Temperance will come up to London.'

'Pru and Hope are already there,' added Chastity. 'And it may be that Jamie will be able to provide assistance.'

'Leave Jamie and Prudence to me,' the Reverend offered hastily. Mercy didn't miss the suspicious glance her stepmother cast his way.

Nate listened to the exchange without speaking. The names meant nothing to him, aside from the small amount Mercy had told him. But actually putting *faces* to names filled him with foreboding. Since returning to England he'd never even been in a room with more than half a dozen people. 'So, just to clarify – I am to be lady Mercedes' bodyguard until Reinhardt shows himself?'

Christian shook his head decisively. 'No, I am expecting far more from you than that. Until such time as Reinhardt is under lock and key, I wish you to put Mercy's safety above all else.'

The two men stared at one other. After a few seconds, the Viscount nodded his understanding.

'May I suggest we go in for dinner now and then perhaps you would be so good as to sleep on it and tell me your decision in the morning. As my wife said earlier, we are entirely cognisant of the enormity of what we are asking, and whatever you decide, I will be forever in your debt.'

'I thought you were never going to suggest it,' Reverend Shackleford grumbled, climbing to his feet. 'I'm fair gutfounded.' He held out his arm for Chastity before adding, 'All this talk of putting a rub in the way of that blackguard Reinhardt has given me an appetite.'

Despite the seriousness of their discussion in the drawing room, dinner actually turned out to be a more lighthearted affair than anyone had anticipated. The Reverend was on fine form, regaling the increasingly incredulous Viscount of the many trials and tribulations he'd been subjected to in the raising of eight daughters. Indeed, he'd only got as far as Patience by the time cheese was being served, having cheerfully informed Nate that the exploits of his fifth daughter would take up an entire dinner alone.

'I really don't think you should be recounting such stories to Nate,' Chastity reprimanded her father with a sigh. 'It will only reinforce his opinion that we are all entirely dicked in the nob.'

'I think he was already of that opinion when Grandmama keeled over in the Black Swan,' Mercy commented with a grin. 'And if he spends any time with the rest of the male members of our family, he will not need the stories. Indeed, Adam declares regularly how traumatised he is, and apparently Max has taken to meditating.' She paused and gave a wicked grin. 'And then of course there's you, Papa...'

Christian gave her a look. 'I think perhaps now would be a good time to ask for the Port,' was all he said drily.

'Do you wish us to leave you to it?' Chastity asked. The Earl shook his head. 'Nate knows our deepest, darkest secrets. I'm certain it's only good manners to keep him at the table...

***

As Mercy lay in her bed going over the events of the evening, a sense of unreality gripped her. The last few days had been surreal. Indeed, it felt as though they'd actually happened to some other version of her.

Putting aside her complex feelings towards the Viscount for a moment, she thought back to her father's comment about Reinhardt wanting something from her mother.

What could it possibly be? She was aware that her mother had been a courtesan, though the Earl had not described her thus in so many words. He'd merely declared that she'd been a friend – but since in Mercy's experience, friends did not generally have children together, it was a logical assumption that her mother had been a doxy.

Not that she would dream of saying that word to her father. If she did, he would lock her up for a month – at the very least. He'd never given Mercy even the slightest reason to be ashamed of her mother, and he regularly declared that the day she'd been left on his doorstep, was one of the two happiest of his life – the other one being the day he married Chastity Shackleford.

Mercedes turned over onto her side. Had her mother left a will? It seemed unlikely. The few trinkets the courtesan had owned had been left in Mercy's coat pocket, with the exception of the locket which she'd been wearing around her neck. Mercy's oldest memory was of her mother telling her never, ever to take it off. The locket had remained around her throat ever since.

She knew her father had tried to discover whether she had any family in Mexico but had given up long before they travelled to England. Mercy certainly didn't feel any urge to learn about her Latin heritage. She was more than content in the bosom of the unconventional family her father had married into.

Swivelling onto her back again, Mercy's thoughts finally turned back to Viscount Carlingford.

Her father's declaration that the truth would be made known

once Reinhardt was out of the picture had changed everything. Both she and Nate would be free to go their separate ways, though in truth, the charade was far more likely to adversely affect her marriage prospects than his. If the Viscount did what was asked of him, he would come out the whole affair a hero and be fighting the ladies off – scar or no scar.

Mercy didn't quite know how that made her feel. He certainly deserved to find happiness, and a wealthy wife would undoubtedly bring him rewards he'd likely never dreamed of.

Including children.

But where did that leave her? Whatever happened, Mercy knew this season would be her last. Suitor or no suitor, she would not be playing the marriage mart again. She would simply turn the problem over to her father who would undoubtedly find her a match. It might not be one made in heaven, but she knew he would do his best to choose someone with whom she could rub comfortably along with.

Was it possible that someone could be Nathaniel Harding…?

***

By the next morning, the snow was completely gone with spring finally returning to the New Forest. Standing at the window, Nate marvelled at the beauty of the scene in front of him. The formal gardens led down to the forest's edge, gradually becoming wilder until they finally merged almost seamlessly. The Viscount knew that Cottesmore had been a smouldering ruin when the Earl first inherited it, and the beauty of the house, and grounds now was a testament to what hard work and money could achieve.

For the first time since he'd stepped foot in Carlingford, Nate wanted the same thing for his own house. He'd been indifferent to his surroundings for so long, this sudden desire to create an actual home was disconcerting to say the least. Part of him was terrified to return to the real world and the fragile hope that happiness was not only to be found in the bottom of a bottle.

But then much would depend on his conversation with the Earl when they met at breakfast. Of course, he would play the part of a besotted fiancé – as Stanhope must have known he would. Nate would do whatever it took to protect Mercy – *whatever* it took.

A small snore came from the bed behind him, pulling him out of his reverie. He turned to regard Ruby with amused exasperation. Though Nate was entirely certain she would live with him on the streets if needs be, the little dog was clearly not averse to the finer things in life, and in truth, Ruby had given him much more than he'd ever given her. But then, hopefully, her loyalty was about to be rewarded.

Yes, he would willingly give his life for Mercedes Stanhope, but first he and the Earl needed to discuss one more condition.

***

The conversation during breakfast was purposely kept to mundane matters such as the uncommon weather after the Earl declared unequivocally that he preferred his bacon and eggs to be business free. This time the whole Stanhope family were present at the table, and Nate found himself holding a conversation with two ten-year-olds for the first time in … well ever. It was certainly an eye opener – especially the questions.

'What did you do to your face?'

'Does it hurt?'

'Will it come off if I touch it?'

'Are you a pirate?'

'I've got a scar like yours.' This from Olivia who had no compunction about hoiking her skirt up to show him the miniscule scar decorating her knee.

'We're going to stay in London while Mercy looks for her husband.'

'I don't know what she's done with him, but he must be very good at hiding.'

'You're not Mercy's husband, are you...?'

'Don't be such a ninnyhammer, Mercy hasn't *lost* her husband, she hasn't found one yet. That's why she's going to look for one.' The scathing comment was from Christopher – or Kit as the rest of the family called him. Clearly the heir to the Earldom, he was a serious boy of around thirteen and fortunately for the future of Cottesmore, nothing at all like his twin sisters.

Before a row could ensue, their mother put down her napkin and rose from her chair. 'I'm certain Miss Horsham will be waiting for you in the school room,' she declared, the tone of her voice more hopeful than anything else. 'So bid Viscount Carlingford goodbye as he will be leaving after breakfast.'

The twins simply waved before chasing each other out of the room. Christopher, however, gave a very creditable bow and politely wished him a safe journey before walking sedately to the door.

'Don't pay too much attention to his impeccable manners,' the Earl murmured drily when the door finally shut behind him. 'If you hadn't been here, he'd have delivered his last remark to his sister alongside a kick.'

'Which would undoubtedly have led to a full-scale battle under the table,' Mercy added. 'Truly you're honoured, my lord. They do not usually show so much interest in a guest.'

'I doubt many of them look like me,' Nate retorted without rancour.

Before Mercy could find a suitable riposte, the door was thrown open again and her grandfather stomped into the room, Flossy trotting happily behind him. 'Have I missed anything?' he demanded, going over to the sideboard to help himself to some devilled kidneys.

'Nothing at all, Augustus,' Christian responded. In fact, as always, you've arrived just as things are hopefully about to get interesting.' He turned towards Nate with raised eyebrows. 'I trust you came to a decision overnight?'

The Viscount automatically glanced over at Mercy. What would she think about what he was about to say? She coloured up under his regard, and for a second, he found himself bereft of words.

Bringing his breakfast back to the table, the Reverend looked at the Viscount in exasperation and muttered, 'Spit it out lad. We haven't got all day.'

Nate gritted his teeth, something he was beginning to realise most people spent much of their time doing when dealing with the clergyman. With difficulty, he forced himself to relax.

'You have my word that I will do everything within my power to ensure Mercedes remains safe,' he said evenly. The Earl closed his eyes in relief, and Nate couldn't help wondering if his lordship would be quite so content after his next words.

'However, I do have one more condition...' Nate left the sentence hanging for a second until he was sure everyone round the table had heard. He watched the Earl glance towards his wife and frown slightly, before turning back and nodding his head in an invitation to speak.

Taking a deep breath, Nate looked over at Mercy as he spoke, knowing it was her reaction he needed to see.

'I wish my betrothal to Mercedes to stand once Reinhardt has been apprehended.' He waited and saw the moment she understood. Her eyes widened and she smothered a gasp. Then, turning back to the Earl, Nate continued, 'As soon as we are certain Mercedes is safe, I would like us to be married.'

Chapter Fifteen

Reinhardt had spent the last week pacing the floor of his lodgings in an agony of impatience. Everything was in position. He had men watching the Earl of Cottesmore's London townhouse round the clock and was confident he'd know the moment his lordship took residence.

In a matter of weeks, he'd be on his way back to Boston and then to Mexico with his new wife.

Throwing himself into a chair, he gave himself over to the pleasurable thought of finally having Mercedes Alfaro's daughter in his clutches. What was even more delicious was the thought that Christian Stanhope had absolutely no idea of the inheritance waiting for his daughter.

Of course, once the chit's identity had been confirmed – and given she was the absolute image of her mother, it shouldn't prove too much of a problem. He had the key, and she had the locket. Indeed, all his sources confirmed that she never removed it.

He felt himself harden as he imagined the young Mercedes in his bed – so much like her mother in every way that mattered. Naturally, the chit wouldn't yet have acquired her mother's skills in the bedroom, but he was looking forward to teaching her exactly what he liked...

***

The Earl of Cottesmore's reaction to what was essentially a request for his daughter's hand in marriage did not include pistols at dawn. In fact, it had to be said his response was remarkably restrained. After regarding Nate silently for a moment, he coolly asked if the Viscount would object to waiting outside as he discussed this latest turn of events with his wife and daughter.

Nate swallowed and nodded, climbing to his feet. 'With your permission my lord, I'll take Ruby for a turn around the garden while I await your decision.' The Earl gave a clipped nod, and Nate abruptly wondered if he was shortly about to be thrown out. Not that he would take his request back. All of a sudden, being able to keep Mercy safe for the rest of her life had become the most important thing in his.

The Reverend, on the other hand, was not quite as reticent. 'Thunder an' turf, Harding, you've got some deuced nerve, I'll give you that.' He bent down, picked up his dog and thrust her unceremoniously into Nate's arms. 'While you're at it, you can give Flossy a walk too.'

The next hour was the longest in the Viscount's entire life. As he walked along the paths meandering towards the Forest edge, he was afraid he'd completely undone the Earl's trust. There was no doubt his demand had been unexpected. Indeed, Stanhope's offer to set him up in society had been more than generous.

But Nate was also well aware that, unexpected or not, there would be no wedding without Mercy's agreement.

Throwing a stick for the two dogs, he ground his teeth in frustration. Was his demand so preposterous? At the end of the day, he was a passable match - if one looked past his hideous face and wretched finances... Abruptly, Nate stopped and seconds later, found himself laughing, though there was nothing humorous in the sound. What the bloody hell had he been thinking? He must have been completely addled to even put such a proposal forward. What possible reason could Mercy have for even considering him for a husband?

'I hardly think our situation cause for amusement, my lord.'

Nate spun round to stare disbelievingly at the subject of his fantasies standing no more than five yards away.

'I ... what are you doing here?' he said, his words coming out more brusquely than he intended.

'I told my father that I needed to speak with you privately before I made my final decision.'

They stared at each other. 'Why do you wish to marry me?' she asked finally in a small voice.

Nate's heart gave a dull thud. 'In truth?' She nodded jerkily. 'The absolute truth is, I don't know,' he bit out. 'All I know is that I've never met anyone like you before.' He threaded his hand through his hair, trying to find the right words. 'I've spent nearly all of my life alone, but no one in their right mind would call it *living*. When you came to Carlingford ... something inside me broke free, and ... and ..., *I can't put it back.*' His whispered voice was tortured, and instinctively she stepped closer.

'I swear I'll take care of you,' he growled. 'I'll never let anyone hurt you... I...' He stopped, the words he wanted so badly to say dying in his throat.

'Will you love me?' Mercy asked softly, cocking her head to one side.

There was a silence. Then, 'I don't know how.' Nate's whisper was anguished.

'Then perhaps we can teach each other.' It was a few seconds before her response sank in and when it did, Nate closed his eyes, fighting the sudden ridiculous onset of tears.

When he opened them again, her softness had vanished. 'I will tell my father that I agree to your terms, providing the problem with Reinhardt has been dealt with.'

'And if it hasn't?'

She quirked a mocking brow. 'If it hasn't, then I think it likely one or both of us will be dead.'

***

The Earl rented a small discreet townhouse for his new son-in-law to be in a pleasant square close to Green Park. Once installed, his valet was dispatched with strict instructions to ensure that the Viscount looked every inch the wealthy aristocrat by the time the rest of them arrived in London, which with luck would be around the middle of May.

Much to Nate's consternation, however, he'd been in London for only two days before the Earl and Countess of Ravenstone arrived, together with their family and entourage. Within hours, the Viscount had received a note *inviting* him to dinner.

Sitting with the summons on his lap, Nate felt as though he was trapped inside a runaway carriage with no driver. Somewhere in the last two weeks, he'd completely lost control of his life, and he had no one to blame but himself. The fact that the Earl of Cottesmore had no intention of making things easy for him had become quickly apparent. And to be honest, who could blame him?

Nate had hardly left the house since he arrived, and currently, just the mere thought of being in his father's world had him wanting to throw himself out of the nearest window. Nevertheless, if he was to protect Mercy as he'd promised, he had to start bloody well acting like *Viscount Carlingford*. A sudden clang of the doorbell pulled him out of his doom-laden thoughts. Glancing down at his brand-new pocket watch, he saw it was nearly midday. Which he'd swiftly learned was far too early for callers – not that there'd been any.

He looked towards the drawing room door, waiting for the butler who'd been rented along with the house to come and tell him who had the temerity to make a call at such an ungodly hour. In the end though, he didn't need an announcement, as the dulcet tones of Reverend Shackleford came floating from the hallway.

'Don't give me any of that nonsense about the Viscount not receiving visitors. I know he's likely been up and about since well before sunup, so be a good man and tell him we're here.'

We're here? Who the bloody hell is we?

Nate hurriedly climbed to his feet. Ruby lifted her head but didn't move from her position in front of the fire. He wasn't the only one overawed by their current situation.

Seconds later, the door opened to reveal the stony-faced butler. 'You have visitors, my lord,' he said in the same tone he'd doubtless use to say, 'You have the plague.'

'Thank you, Grimsby. Perhaps you would be so good as to ask Mrs. Lovell to bring us some tea.' The butler gave a frosty bow, and withdrew, leaving the doorway clear for the Reverend ... and two strangers, one of which looked no older than eight or nine. Entirely forgetting his role as the courteous master of the house, Nate regarded them silently for a second before saying flatly, 'A little notice wouldn't have gone amiss.'

'What did you want – a four-piece orchestra?' The Reverend's response was equally ill-mannered, and strangely enough, it served to finally break the sense of coming disaster that had gripped Nate since he'd arrived.

'Ah didnae ken ye haed a dog, Maister.' The boy's delight was entirely unfeigned as he hurried over to Ruby and got down onto his hands and knees making clucking noises. Naturally, the terrier immediately rolled onto her back.

'Where's Flossy?' asked Nate, suddenly realising the clergyman's ever-present companion was missing.

'With Lilyanna.' At Nate's enquiring look, he added, 'Temperance and Adam's youngest.' He didn't elaborate but his pained look said it all. The Viscount turned towards the Reverend's companion, a small, slightly weasel-faced man with a single tuft of sandy coloured hair sticking out of his scalp. He too was wearing a cassock, marking him a man of the cloth.

'My curate, Percy,' the Reverend stated, 'and the lad on the floor is his son, Finn.'

'I'm very pleased to meet you, my lord,' the curate murmured, executing a clumsy bow. Nate inclined his head in return.

'You don't need to stand on ceremony with this fellow, Percy lad. Trust me, his house is worse than yours.'

Fortunately, at that moment, the housekeeper returned with a tray of tea.

'Dae ye hae any tablet, Missus?' asked Finn from the floor.

Since the boy might as well have been speaking French, the Reverend sighed and asked if she could bring some wafers, before turning to his curate and adding, 'Do you ever feed the lad, Percy?'

Nate didn't ask why the boy had a broad Scottish accent, but presumed he must have been adopted.

'I assume this isn't a social call,' he commented drily to the Reverend instead, waving his guests towards the small sofa.

'Three sugars and plenty of cream in mine,' the clergyman announced as Nate poured out the tea. Gritting his teeth, the

Viscount continued without looking up.

'I thought we'd take the opportunity to have a bit of a tit a tit before my son-in-law arrives,' Augustus Shackleford continued. 'I'm very fond of Christian, but sometimes I think he was born with a poker up his arse. He's worse than Nicholas, and that's saying something.' Nate blinked, for a second having no idea what the clergyman was talking about. Then the curate gave a small cough and mumbled, 'Tête-à-tête,' into his tea.

'That's what I said. When was the last time you washed out your ears, Percy?'

'Mam gies him a clip roond th' ear an 'e misses 'is lughole,' Finn piped up helpfully from the floor, his accent rendered even more difficult to understand with his mouth full of wafer.

For the first time, Nate felt truly bereft of words and abruptly his sense of doom returned a hundredfold.

'I can't imagine what we might have to speak of that cannot be said in front of the Earl,' he retorted stiffly.

Reverend Shackleford looked at him as though he'd suddenly sprouted two heads. 'Well, since your lifetime of happiness might be reduced to mere weeks if Reinhardt gets his way, I thought you'd be interested in helping me and Percy catch the varmint.'

***

'Do you think your fiancé will prefer this colour or this on you, my lady?' Mercy looked at the seamstress in confusion for a second. She still hadn't got used to describing Nathaniel Harding as her husband to be. The whole thing was bizarre, and so far from her comfort level, she sometimes wondered whether some other Mercedes had somehow inhabited her body.

Indeed, whatever romantic notions she'd held for her future most definitely had not included a broken man who had no idea how to love. If she was being entirely honest, they hadn't really included much in the way of romance at all.

Mercy had always believed that love was the natural long-term outcome of mutual respect and, yes, affection. She chose to ignore the fact that nearly every romantic relationship in her family had been intense, tempestuous and passionate from the onset - generally assuring herself that she was possessed of far more common sense than her more volatile relatives.

But the fact of the matter was, she didn't feel the expected respect and affection for Nate Harding. In truth, she didn't really know what she felt. But never in her life had she wanted to kiss a man quite so much. How scandalous was that?

She couldn't share such tumultuous feelings with her stepmother, and she wouldn't be seeing either Jenny or Tory again until the house party at Blackmore. She didn't actually know what to do with such longings. But it wasn't only that. A hitherto hardly thought about area between her legs throbbed whenever she thought about him touching her. Truly, it was most uncomfortable.

Why she should feel so about a man whose face most people found difficult to look at, she had no idea, but she found herself wanting to trace the scar down his cheek with her fingers and kiss the puckered flesh. Was she addled?

Had it been the same for others in her family? She'd seen firsthand that Jennifer and Brendon couldn't keep their hands off one another. What about her father and stepmother? Mercy found herself remembering her first meeting with Chastity Shackleford. For a reason lost to the annals of time, both she and the Reverend had been trying to climb into her father's bedchamber via a tree outside his window. Why the devil had she never asked why?

Mercy found herself chuckling inside. Surely that proved her father's relationship with his wife was not devoid of passion – and then there was the fevered kisses she'd seen them exchange when they thought no one was looking...

So mayhap she wasn't quite so different to everyone else in her family after all. For some reason, the notion gave her an unexpected comfort.

She became aware that the seamstress was speaking again and forced her thoughts back to the task at hand. Despite her confusion and uncertainty, she couldn't deny her relief that this would be the last time she'd need a whole new wardrobe designed purely to impress a section of the population who for the most part possessed nothing between their ears but fresh air. However, the relief was swiftly followed by the sobering hope that it wouldn't be because she'd fallen into the clutches of a madman...

Chapter Sixteen

By the time Mercy arrived in London, Viscount Carlingford's presence, as well as his disfigurement were both common knowledge. The fact that he was apparently betrothed to Lady Mercedes Stanhope however, was still causing a stir.

For the most part, the gossips fell into three camps: Those who felt wholly sorry for the bride to be, given that she'd have to indulge in ... *you know what*... with someone so disfigured. Those who were envious and spiteful since they considered the Viscount's bank balance and title to be of much more interest than his lack of a pretty face. And thirdly, those who found the thought of being intimate with someone quite so *gothic* deliciously thrilling...

On his arrival in London, Christian had immediately put the Viscount's name forward for White's. While Adam would willingly have done so already, it was felt that Mercy's father being the one doing the proposing would send the right signals to the rest of the *ton*. Thus, on the night of his fiancée's arrival, Nate found himself attending the exclusive club with two earls, a marquess, another viscount and a magistrate. For a man who six weeks earlier had been poaching his dinner, it all felt like a bag of moonshine.

However, he quickly realised that these men who'd won the hearts of the fabled Shackleford Sisters were no society poodles. They clearly had a close bond that they made no effort to hide.

Nate's dinner at the Earl of Ravenstone's residence had gone surprisingly well. In fact, most of his interrogation had been conducted by the Countess, who'd seemed less interested in what he looked like, and more in how he intended to treat her niece. Naturally, the subject of Reinhardt had also come up, but any in-depth discussion had been put aside until the Earl of Cottesmore's arrival.

In fairness, his nerves on arrival at the club were much less than he'd previously feared. Most men present had no real interest in his scar, unless it was to pat him on the back for taking one on the chin against old Boney, and for the most part their group was left alone at their customary table in the corner.

'Have you heard from Nick?' Gabriel, Viscount Northwood asked when their wine had been poured.

Christian nodded. 'He assured me that he and Grace will be here by the month's end.'

'Is our American friend likely to wait that long before he makes his move?' The Marquis of Guildford looked sceptical.

Christian grimaced. 'I really don't know, Max. I haven't laid eyes on the bastard since before I left New York. I'd have thought that after his first attempt failed, he'll want to be very sure of success before he tries again.'

'I have men watching out for an American matching Reinhardt's description,' Jamie Fitzroy, their resident magistrate informed them, 'but as I see it, our two most pressing problems are that, firstly, while we think his motive is to force Mercy into wedlock, we don't really know why, and secondly is there a time constraint on him achieving whatever it is that he wants? If we can discover either, it will help us predict his movements.'

'I assume we're working on the theory that the more desperate he is, the more likely he is to make a mistake.' Nate surprised himself with his comment, though he was even more startled at his lack of deference in the presence of such exulted company – as well as their complete lack of condescension as they considered his comment.

'Is there any way of finding out just what he's after?' Gabriel asked. 'I mean we know that Mercy's a beautiful woman and a prime catch, but America's a bloody long way and I'd have thought there were plenty of wealthy heiresses waiting to be fleeced by an ivory turner such as Reinhardt.' Nate realised the Earl must have shared the story of how he'd come to know Reinhardt with all of them.

'There's something he's after,' agreed Christian. 'I've spent hours thinking back to the days leading up to Mercy's mother's death, and I've come to the conclusion that she had something Reinhardt wanted. At first, I imagined she'd stolen something belonging to him, but if that was the case, why would he need Mercy?' He shook his head.

'The more I think about it, the more I think there was more to Mercy's mother than I ever realised. She never told me her family name, and I never had any success locating anyone who knew it, though I confess I didn't try particularly hard. I assumed she'd been brought up on the streets, but since her English was at best broken, there was no way of knowing whether her family back in Mexico were poverty-stricken or not.'

He looked round at his silent companions. 'What if they weren't? What if her family had been wealthy? She could have run away for a hundred different reasons.' He paused, gathering his thoughts.

'I think Reinhardt knew her name, and I think he knew who her family were.'

'You believe Mercy has an inheritance waiting for her.' Adam's words were not phrased as a question.

Christian nodded. 'I do. The more I think about it, it's the only thing that makes sense.'

'So, if Reinhardt marries Mercy, what's hers becomes his.' Max shook his head in disgust.

'If that's the case,' Nate commented levelly, 'then he's going to be all the more desperate to put an end to our engagement.' He looked round at the men surrounding him - friends he'd never thought he'd have – and added, 'So if we wish to put an end to this, I suggest we give the bastard a compelling reason to show his hand.'

***

'Jamie already has men on the lookout for this Reinhardt, based on the description you gave the sketch artist,' Prudence told her father. 'I'm not sure what else he can do.'

'Well, for a start, the fellow's not British,' Reverend Shackleford answered. 'Are there any eating or lodging houses that favour visitors from the Americas? If there are, they'd likely be near the docks.'

'I'm certain he'll have thought of that, Father. And I really don't think London Docks are quite the place for you and Percy.'

'Tare an' hounds girl, who are you and what have you done with Prudence?'

'She's the mother of two young children,' his daughter responded tartly.

'Well, now you know how deuced difficult it is,' the Reverend hmphed, entirely without sympathy.

Prudence pursed her lips. Deep inside, she was aware that she'd recently lost a little of what made her ... well, whatever it was that made her Pru - exchanging monsters for household ledgers and ghost stories for gossip sheets. Though, in truth, this was the first time she'd had it pointed out to her. Did Jamie miss the old Pru? He never said.

Frowning, she stood up to pour the tea. 'It would take weeks to visit every lodging house, pub and eating house – not to mention the dozens of brothels and dolly shops,' she declared brusquely. 'You'd have better luck finding a needle in a haystack.'

She handed the Reverend his tea and sat back down. For a second, she was silent, then gave a small cough before saying a trifle defensively, 'Mayhap I could make one or two enquiries. I know our cook's nephew works at London Docks. Perhaps he'll know of somewhere that favours travellers to and from the Americas. I assume Reinhardt will be looking for passage once he's managed to abduct Mercy?'

'If he's got any sense, he'll already have it booked,' her father grunted. 'And if he has, there should be a record of it.'

Prudence sipped her tea thoughtfully. 'I'm certain Jamie already has men enquiring about ships bound for Boston or New York within the next few weeks. Though if the scoundrel's already booked passage, I doubt he'll have used his own name.'

She paused for a second before seemingly making her mind up. 'You'll need to give me twenty-four hours. That should give the cook enough time to speak with her nephew.' She put down her dish and looked over at her father sternly. 'If I so much as suspect you and Percy have been wandering London Docks before then, so help me, I'll have Jamie lock you both up in the nearest cell.'

Hiding his sudden excitement, the Reverend nodded solemnly, saying, 'Crook my elbow and wish it never comes straight,' while crossing his fingers behind his back. In truth, he was thinking if he got back quick enough, he, Percy and Finn could head towards the docks this afternoon. He'd offer his apologies upstairs as soon as they had Oliver Reinhardt under lock and key.

'You'll send me a message as soon as you've got something?' he asked nonchalantly, climbing to his feet.

Prudence looked at him narrowly. She might not be as reckless as she once was, but that didn't mean she was bacon brained enough not to recognise when her father was shamming it.

She stood up in turn, still eying him closely. 'I'll send word. In the meantime, please try to stay out of trouble, Father.'

The Reverend gave her a wounded look but thought it best to scarper before he was forced to tell an even bigger plumper. The Almighty might forgive him one, but in the Reverend's experience, things tended to go very quickly to hell in a handcart if he tried to get away with two in the same conversation...

***

Pulling on her gloves and placing her bonnet over her artfully contrived curls, Mercy examined herself in the mirror. She was surprised to see how calm and serene she looked. Inside, she was almost shaking with excitement.

Today she was to see Nate again for the first time in over a month. Instead of lessening as she'd believed it might, the strange restlessness every time she thought of him had actually increased. The ache between her legs had been keeping her awake at night, so much so that she was beginning to wonder if there was something wrong with her. Indeed, in the depths of the night, after waking covered in a light film of perspiration, Mercy decided that at the very least she was going to have to somehow get him to kiss her. If that didn't put an end to the throbbing, then she very much feared she'd have to persuade her father to allow the wedding to take place as soon as possible.

How she was going to achieve such a thing surrounded by half a dozen chaperones, Mercy had no idea. Mayhap the answer was to simply plant herself onto his lap and press her lips to his. That it would achieve the desired result she had no doubt.

With a small giggle, she picked up her reticule, feeling lighter than she had since she'd left Scotland. As she made her way downstairs, for the first time, she forgot entirely about Reinhardt.

Nate arrived at exactly four p.m. As he was shown into the drawing room, Mercy drew in her breath. She hadn't seen him looking all the crack before and hadn't suspected he had such a magnificent physique. The scar on his face, instead of making him repulsive, somehow added to his allure, giving him a roguish air. *Like a pirate*, she thought remembering her sister's comment at Cottesmore. Her heart was beating so loud she thought he must hear it as he bent to lift her hand to his lips.

'You have changed, my lord,' she murmured breathlessly. He lifted his eyes and stared at her, his gaze suddenly hot and intent.

'You have not, my lady,' he answered finally, hoarsely.

Mercy glanced at her stepmother, grateful Chastity was looking discreetly out of the window so missed her sudden blush.

'Shall we?' At the Viscount's invitation, Chastity finally turned and gave him a warm smile.

'Tempy and Hope are meeting us with the girls at the entrance to Kensington Gardens,' she said, pulling on her gloves.

Ordinarily Mercy would have been delighted to see her cousins, Roseanna, Francesca and Lilyanna, but that would make their party eight for goodness' sake. 'Is Papa coming along too?' she couldn't help asking caustically, wondering if she should suggest a partridge in a pear tree.

Chastity grinned at her stepdaughter in complete understanding. Nate on the other hand thought she was referring to the feeling of safety her father provided. 'Reinhardt will never show his face if you are surrounded by too many gentlemen,' he reminded her gently. 'You have no cause for concern, my lady. I will not leave your side.'

His words brought Mercy back down to earth with a bump. Biting her lip, she took his proffered arm and allowed him to lead her outside to the waiting barouche.

Once there, she immediately spied his horse at the front of the four horses champing at their bits. 'Duchess,' she exclaimed happily, pulling off her gloves and going over to stroke the mare.

'I couldn't leave her behind,' Nate explained with a chuckle. 'Although judging by the bite marks on her three companions, she doesn't work well in a team.'

Mercy laughed, 'And where is Ruby?'

'With my housekeeper, Mrs. Lovell,' he told her. 'She's been collecting admirers since she trotted through the door and was perfectly happy keeping a watchful eye on the slow roasting beef. The greedy madam has never eaten so well, and in truth, *three* novices promenading in Hyde Park was simply too much.'

'Who's the third one?' Mercy quipped as he helped her into the barouche.

'You have to ask?' he deadpanned. 'Be grateful your father provided me with a driver. If it was me controlling the horses, we'd undoubtedly end up in the Serpentine.' With Mercy settled, he assisted Chastity into the carriage, then seated himself opposite. Seconds later, they were clattering out of the square.

***

'Right then, Percy, I suggest we start with the Eastern Dock. According to this map, it's the smaller of the two.'

'Where did you get the map from, Sir?'

The Reverend frowned at his curate. 'Of all the questions you could have asked, that's the one you come up with?'

'We gaun tae see some ships then Revren?' Finn's response was clearly more to the clergyman's liking and he grinned down at the excited boy.

'That we are lad. Go and fetch your coat and we'll be off.'

Finn needed no further urging. After hurriedly helping himself to an extra piece of bread which he stuffed into his pocket *for later*, he ran off to his bedchamber.

Percy sighed as he watched the boy go. 'I don't think he'll ever get used to the idea that his next meal is assured,' he murmured before turning to his superior and adding sternly, 'Sir, you really shouldn't be stuffing his head full of nonsense. I'm not sure he should even be accompanying us. The docks are no place for an impressionable lad.'

The Reverend regarded Percy with something approaching pity. 'Well, just you try and tell him he's got to stay here,' the clergyman suggested. 'I predict the boy'll be following us within five minutes. At least this way we get to keep an eye on him. And don't forget it was your deuced idea to bring him to London in the first place.'

'Finn's too much of a handful for Lizzy on her own,' Percy sighed, 'and I thought we'd have the chance to see the sights.'

'You are – you're seeing London Docks,' Augustus Shackleford retorted. 'It'll be a damn sight more useful to him than showing him a few dandies mincing down Bond Street.'

Ten minutes later, they were climbing into the Earl of Cottesmore's second best carriage.

'Will his lordship object to us using his carriage without permission?' Percy asked as they headed out onto the busy street.

'He wasn't here to ask,' the Reverend retorted, lifting Flossy onto his lap. 'But I'm certain that if he knew what we were about, he'd be more than happy to give his blessing.' The clergyman finished with a small self-conscious cough. Even Finn had looked doubtful at that bag of moonshine.

It didn't take long to reach the entrance to the Eastern docks, and after requesting the coach driver return for them in two hours, Reverend Shackleford attached Flossy to her lead and headed into the seething mass surrounding London Docks.

Chapter Seventeen

If Mercy had had any concerns that their barouche would not attract sufficient attention, she was quickly disabused of the notion. Indeed, it took them a whole hour and a half to arrive at the entrance to Kensington Gardens. Initially, most people's eyes slid on and off her betrothed – clearly, they were macabrely intrigued but entirely discomfited to display such a bourgeois reaction. In the end, Nate himself took to referring directly to his disfigurement, making the inevitable *Beauty and the Beast* jest and scandalously declaring that not only did he have a good heart and generous spirit, but many other attributes that might fascinate a young woman of discerning taste. In the end, Mercy thought that if she never heard another titter in her life, it would be too soon.

That they'd achieved what they'd set out to do was without question - their betrothal would undoubtedly be society's main topic for weeks to come - which meant that Reinhardt couldn't fail to hear about it.

And while Mercy found herself feeling somewhat vulnerable and exposed as she climbed down from the carriage to greet her aunts and cousins, she also felt a good deal of female satisfaction that such an intriguing man actually belonged to her.

Ten minutes later, she was back to gritting her teeth. Had Roseanna and Francesca always been so witty and attractive? And why hadn't she noticed that Lilyanna's ebony curls owed nothing to artifice? Her own hair might well be the same colour, but that was where the similarity ended. In truth, without curling irons, her own tresses resembled a horse's tail.

And as for stealing a kiss – there would be more chance of her becoming the next queen of England.

Any minute now she'd be stamping her foot in temper...

This wouldn't do. Mercy took a deep breath as she watched Nate courteously hand her Aunt Hope a glass of lemonade obtained from a vendor at the entrance to the gardens. Since when had she become such a crosspatch? Calling a spade a spade was one thing, but wanting to hit someone over the head with one...

While her betrothed handed refreshments to all their company, Mercy made a concerted effort to quash her peevishness. When he was finished, she stepped forward and determinedly tucked her arm in his. He looked down at her enquiringly and she didn't know whether to be happy or sad that he was already picking up on her moods. In the end she offered a tentative smile and sipped at the lemonade she held in her free hand.

'Do you think he's here now, watching us?' Hope couldn't completely hide her anxiety as they finished their refreshments.

'I doubt very much he would risk showing himself,' Nate responded firmly. 'While I didn't actually see him at the inn, he doesn't know that. My guess is that he will stay hidden in the shadows until such time as he can make his move.'

'We're certainly grateful for your protection my lord,' Francesca commented coquettishly, sending all Mercy's good intentions sailing away in the wind.

'I'm entirely certain if we stay together, we are in no danger,' Chastity declared firmly.

'If he's bottle-headed enough to try and snatch Mercy in the presence of so many witnesses, then he's certainly not the threat we're imagining him to be.' As always Temperance's comments were succinct and to the point. 'That he has *someone* watching us, I've no doubt. So, we must need goad him to the point where he will do something foolish.'

She proved her point by laughing gaily and saying in a loud voice, 'Lord Carlingford, you are incorrigible. I swear I'm awaiting your marriage to my niece with as much trepidation as anticipation. Has the date for the nuptials been set yet?'

After giving her a level look, Nate played along. 'Alas, it's out of my hands.' He gave an adoring look down towards Mercy, causing her to blush, even though she knew it was for their possible audience. 'I cannot wait to make Mercedes my bride and it's my dearest hope that her father won't insist that we wait until the end of the season to make it official.' He looked enquiringly over at Chastity, who took up the challenge.

'I have already spoken with my lord husband,' she trilled, 'and begged him not to stand in the way of such obvious affection. It's my fervent hope he'll give his blessing for the wedding to take place before the middle of June.'

Squeals and hugs all round completed the charade and if Mercy was heard to mutter, 'And if he believes that Canterbury tale, he'll believe anything,' then it was only by those in the very immediate vicinity.

***

'So, exactly what are we looking for, Sir?' Percy shouted as they stared in awe at the multitude of quays and jetties stretching as far as the eye could see. In between were warehouses and sheds, and beyond, line after line of vast leviathans, their masts and riggings visible even over the top of the warehouses.

As they hovered at the entrance to the nearest quay, Finn stared at the closest ship in awestruck silence as a sailor climbed up the rigging like a monkey to hang fearlessly over the deck, so far below. The cacophony of noise around them was so loud it was difficult to hold a conversation. Food vendors were hawking everything from oysters to hot cross buns and only swift footedness stopped them being run over by carts piled high with unloaded goods. Groups of sailors, clearly heading for the nearest pub or brothel, laughed and jostled one another, their language so ripe, Percy was tempted to cover Finn's ears.

'And this is the smaller dock,' Reverend Shackleford murmured, uncharacteristically intimidated.

"Miss Prudence was right, Sir. It will take us all day and night to explore every establishment, and in truth, I wouldn't wish to be here when it begins to get dark.'

The Reverend looked at his curate in irritation. 'Tare an' hounds, Percy, I've had custards with more spine than you. We can't just give up at the first hurdle.'

'So where do you suggest we start then?' the small man answered, taking no offence at the Reverend's blunt assessment of his character. Since reading *The Illustrated Art To Manliness,* a few years earlier, Percy was much more sanguine when it came to his superior's slights, finding the simple repeating of, *'The path to inner peace is by ignoring mutton heads,'* under his breath whilst stroking his right ear was often enough to subdue the urge to hit the Reverend over the head with the nearest Bible.

Augustus Shackleford picked up Flossy and turned in a slow circle. 'What about that pub over there?' He pointed to a large establishment about fifty yards away. Predictably it was named *the Ship in Dock.* Percy eyed it critically - it appeared in quite good repair, and its position would likely mean it saw plenty of trade. Hopefully, they'd find something useful.

Calling Finn to him, he followed his superior towards the entrance, trying hard to quash the ever-present sense of imminent doom that generally accompanied any outing with the Reverend.

***

Mercy was uncharacteristically silent on the journey back to the town house, so much so that Chastity looked at her in concern. As the barouche finally stopped outside, she wondered if she should invite the Viscount in for refreshment, or whether her stepdaughter would perhaps prefer to be alone with her thoughts.

In the event, Mercedes herself declared – quite forcefully, it had to be said - that she believed some tea would finish off a splendid afternoon and would his lordship do her the honour of sitting for a while in the garden.

If Nate was surprised at her offer, he didn't show it. Merely inclined his head with a smile and replied that he'd be delighted.

Chastity however, had alarm bells ringing in her head loud enough to rival those at St. Mary Le Bow, especially when Mercy suggested solicitously that since it was merely the garden, there was surely no necessity for a chaperone.

As Chastity hovered uncertainly at the bottom of the stairs, Mercy played her trump card. 'Stepmama, why don't you take this opportunity to rest for a while? The twins will undoubtedly be back with Miss Horsham very soon.'

Her words served a dual purpose. Firstly, the thought of the twins rampaging through the house was enough to want to make anyone want to lie down while the going was good, and secondly knowing the twins would be rampaging through the house shortly would undoubtedly put her stepmother's mind at rest at the thought of leaving her and Nate alone together.

In truth, it simply told Mercy there was no time to waste...

A few minutes later she and Nate were seated on a bench in a nicely secluded arbour redolent with the scent of honeysuckle. While they were waiting for the tea to be delivered, Mercy smoothed her hair, then smoothed her dress, then smoothed her gloves. Then she eyed the back of the house anxiously, wondering whether they could be seen from any of the windows.

'Are you feeling out of sorts, my lady?' Nate's enquiry came as quite a shock. For a few seconds she'd forgotten he was there. She fought the urge to laugh. Here she was, so engaged in plucking up the courage to kiss him that she'd actually forgotten his presence.

She gave a small cough and smoothed her dress again. 'No indeed, my lord... I was merely...' she paused observing with relief the arrival of a footman with their tea. Nodding to him in thanks, Mercy wondered almost hysterically if her intention was showing on her face – did she look wanton perchance? What did wanton actually look like? Was he even now running to tattle to Mrs. Lovell?

'Would you like me to pour?' Mercy swallowed, casting a sideways glance at the Viscount who was regarding her with concern. It was hardly surprising since she was behaving like a complete goosecap. Knowing it was now or never, she shifted abruptly to face him, her heart slamming against her ribs. She licked her lips, then before she had the chance to change her mind, threw herself forward, and flung her hands around his neck, pressing her lips against his.

Unfortunately, her attempted seduction didn't quite have the effect she was hoping for. Indeed, her tackle was so vigorous, she caught a brief panic-stricken expression on his face just before he toppled backwards off the bench, taking her with him.

Mercy barely had time to utter a small scream before they landed with a thud directly behind the bench, wedged in as tightly as pilchards in a barrel.

***

Before entering the pub, Reverend Shackleford turned towards his curate with a couple of last-minute instructions. 'Now remember, Percy if things get nasty, just threaten to excommunicate the varmints.'

'We're not Catholics, Sir, we don't have the authority.'

'I doubt they'll know the difference. I should think the last time any of these varlets went to church was in leading strings and the next time'll be in a deuced box.' Tucking Flossy under his arm, he pushed open the door.

The inside of the pub was dim and pungent with the smell of tallow from the few candles high up on the walls. The Reverend waited for a few moments to allow his eyes to adjust, then he stepped forward and looked round.

Despite the early evening rowdiness outside, the pub was actually relatively quiet. There were quite a few patrons, though nowhere near as many as one might expect for early evening. Those that were seated were clearly high-ranking ship's officers and nearly all were eating alone and minding their own business.

The Reverend's heart sank. It was the kind of place that fleeced a man of half his belongings for a bit of dried-up steak that may or may not have come from something dead. They should have investigated a little further rather than picking on the first place they spied. He was unlikely to glean anything useful from such a pretentious establishment.

'Can I get you anything, Father?' Flossy gave a low growl in the Reverend's arms.

The Reverend jumped. 'Certainly, my good man,' he responded jovially after pulling himself together. In truth, he may have done it a little too brown since his voice was so cheery, Finn was looking at him in astonishment, muttering, 'be the Revren some ither bodie?'

'My companion and I would like two tankards of your best ale.' The Reverend smiled genially, hoping he actually had enough coin on him to pay. He felt a trickle of sweat down his back. None of the other patrons looked up. It was nothing at all like the Red Lion back in Blackmore and he felt a sudden jolt of homesickness.

Meanwhile, Flossy was making no bones about her opinion of the man behind the bar and was now busy baring her teeth. Turning to Finn, the Reverend hurriedly handed over the little dog and directed the lad to a secluded corner before dragging Percy towards the bar.

Once there, he waited until the first tankard had been filled before giving a small self-conscious cough and saying pleasantly, 'You must be very accustomed to visitors from all corners of the globe here.' The barman looked up at him for a second without speaking and the Reverend added a hasty, 'my son,' in the hope of reminding the man he was speaking to a man of the cloth.

In the end, the barman nodded, sliding the tankard towards Percy. 'We're an exclusive establishment here, Reverend...' he let his sentence trail off, clearly waiting for a little more information.

'Sinclair,' the Reverend responded graciously, endeavouring to give the impression that in addition to being God's representative, he was also a man of the world. 'And this is my curate Percival.' Finally getting into his stride, he finished by giving a slightly condescending inclination of his head – just enough to give the impression he was someone the barman would be unwise to offend.

'Naturally we have visitors from overseas,' the barman

responded carefully, sliding the second tankard across.

'Dae ye hae any pickled eggs?' Finn shouted hopefully from the corner. The boy had recently been introduced to the snack and pronounced his life changed forever. The Reverend gritted his teeth.

'Do you get many passengers coming from the Americas?'

The barman eyed him narrowly. 'Why do you want to know?'

'I have a cousin in Boston,' the Reverend answered without missing a beat. 'I received a missive from him yesterday informing me he was about to embark on a ship to London. Unfortunately, the letter is two months old, and I've no idea which ship he was sailing on.'

'We don't get many here from the West,' the barman answered, giving the bar a cursory mop with a rag that despite his claims to be an upmarket establishment, looked as though he'd found it in the gutter. 'They mostly come from the other way.' He nodded his head towards his approximation of what constituted East.

For a second the Reverend thought he wouldn't say anything else, until he added, 'If it's the Americas you're interested in, you'll need to ask at *the Sail Loft*. It's a lodging house over in the Tobacco Dock'

Chapter Eighteen

Staring down at the Viscount, her face the colour of a ripe tomato, Mercy wondered if she would ever be able to look him in the eyes again. Until, finally, she allowed herself to *really look* at him, and all thought fled.

He made no move to extract them both, but simply raised his hand to brush a stray lock of hair that had fallen to lay on his cheek. With a start, she realised that there was hardness pressing insistently between her legs and she fought the urge to instinctively grind herself against it. Her nipples were like hard pebbles, and they were tingling in a most disconcerting way.

Mesmerised, she stared into his golden eyes, heavy lidded and fixed *entirely* on her. After what seemed like forever, he gave a low groan which her body responded to with a trickle of moisture in that secret part of her. Then he raised his hand to grip the back of her head, pulling her inexorably towards him.

Her hands were still around his neck, gripping the hair at his nape. A distant part of her wondered if she should be resisting, struggling to get off him and back to her feet, but even as the thought came, she dismissed it. In truth, if hell had her, she could have not pulled away.

At long, long last, his lips were less than an inch away and without taking his eyes from hers, he raised his other hand to stroke his thumb across her mouth, until with an incoherent murmur, he threaded both hands into the hair at her temple and pulled again, until her lips finally, *finally* touched his. The barest whisper.

She'd never imagined they would be so soft... until they weren't. His groan wasn't low this time, but almost tortured. He held her still as his lips plundered hers, drinking their sweetness like a drowning man. Instinctively, she opened her mouth, tangling her tongue with his, unconsciously making a soft whimpering sound as she tried to somehow press herself into him.

And then his left hand slid from her head and slipped in between them. Without thinking, Mercy lifted her upper body, automatically giving access to his seeking fingers. With the briefest of pauses, his hand slid over her left breast, cupping it in its entirety, giving relief at long last to the ache that had so plagued her. Wildly she wondered how it could get any better than this, but when his other hand slid to cup her other breast and his thumbs finally brushed against her erect nipples, she cried out against his mouth, her whole body spasming.

Her soft cry brought Nate to his senses. Dear God, what the bloody hell was he doing? He snatched his hands from her breasts and gripped her shoulders to hold her still while he tried to get himself under control. For a second, Mercy resisted, instinctively pushing against his vice like grip, until he ground out hoarsely, 'Mercedes, we have to stop, *now.*'

Blinking, she gazed down at him, still in the grip of feelings she'd never even imagined existed. Then, slowly her face suffused with colour as humiliation crept in and she tried to extract herself.

'Don't.' His voice was harsh, and she stopped, looking down at him in sudden fear. 'Don't,' he repeated, this time softly. Seconds later, he took a deep breath, and pushed her gently until she was sitting astride him. Gritting his teeth at the feel of her softness against that part of him that needed her the most, Nate finally managed to sit upright.

For long seconds they stared at each other. 'Forgive me,' he said softly. Mercy simply shook her head and lifted her hand to touch his scar as she'd wanted to do for so long. Wordlessly, she traced the puckered line down towards his jawbone. Though he stiffened, Nate didn't try to stop her. Tears pricked at her eyes at the agonies he must have suffered over so many years.

But no more. She would love him until the last breath left her body.

She suppressed an instinctive gasp as sudden realisation gripped her. This wasn't simply an infatuation. She loved Nate Harding with all her heart and soul. She had no idea when it had happened, but she knew, with a certainty that transcended all common sense, that he was meant to be hers.

And she was meant to be his.

Mercy didn't resist as he placed his hands underneath her arms and lifted her up towards the bench until she was finally able to get her feet back underneath her.

It took minutes more for Nate to extract himself from the bushes they'd fallen into and by the time he managed to climb back onto the bench, he collapsed with a soft expletive.

'Tea, my lord?' she asked when he finally looked over at her.

He lifted his brows and regarded her impassively for a few seconds, until abruptly they both burst into a peal of laughter.

***

'The *bastard*,' Reinhardt swore softly. The news that Mercedes Stanhope was all of a sudden betrothed had come as a complete shock. He had no doubt that the hurried engagement had been arranged after his abortive kidnapping attempt. Likely to keep him from trying again. Did Stanhope know about her inheritance?

Climbing to his feet, Reinhardt poured himself a brandy, his thoughts a maelstrom of anger, fear and sheer desperation. If the Earl did know, how the devil had he found out? Swallowing the fiery liquid in one gulp, Reinhardt gripped the glass tightly, only just managing to quash the urge to smash it against the wall.

Stanhope couldn't possibly know.

Gritting his teeth, Reinhardt poured himself another drink. That he'd brought this on himself with his ill-considered gamble in Corsham only fuelled his anger. When he finally got his hands on the bitch, she'd pay, oh, how she'd pay.

But the fact remained that the option of taking his time and lulling Stanhope into a false sense of security had gone out of the window. He needed to act *now*. Which meant taking a risk. His plan to sail on The *Windward* in six weeks' time was also no longer possible. He needed to buy passage on The *Western Star* which he knew was leaving in two days.

Reinhardt turned to Davy, standing nervously near to the door, clearly fearing the American's reaction to the news of his quarry's sudden betrothal.

'Find out what she's doing over the next twenty-four hours. I want to know any plans that involve her leaving the house. And warn off the priest. Tell him to be ready to get his drunken arse to the docks.' He swallowed the rest of his brandy and slammed his glass onto the tray. 'Tell Tess I'm going to need the room from tonight. She's to take no other lodgers until I've wed the bitch and we're on board the ship. You'll get your money before we sail - I suggest you take it and run – as far and as fast as you can.

'The Earl of Cottesmore doesn't forgive or forget.'

***

Nate looked at himself in the mirror. It was the first time he'd done so in years. Then he touched the scar, tracing the path Mercy's fingers had taken earlier. What the hell did she see in him? Why didn't his disfigurement repulse her?

He thought back to their impromptu *encounter* earlier and immediately felt himself going hard. He had no doubt that she'd wanted him. He saw again the look on her face as he'd stroked her nipples. If he'd yanked up her skirts and delved between her legs, he knew she'd have been more than ready for him. Why? It didn't make any sense.

He hadn't had sex in… bloody hell, he really couldn't remember – only that he'd paid for it. And now, all of a sudden, he had a beautiful woman actually *panting* for him.

He gave a harsh laugh. His face certainly hadn't improved since he'd last looked at it, but for whatever reason, Mercedes Stanhope saw something that no one else did.

And it terrified him.

She saw past his scars – the ones inside as well as the one on his face – and even knowing just how broken he was, she wanted him anyway.

What if he let her down? He'd never had anyone in his life that he truly cared about. He didn't know how to have a relationship or even how to be close to someone. His heart had been closed for so long - shutting himself off had been the only way to survive the loneliness - and now a large part of him believed he was no longer capable of any deep feelings.

But that was until earlier today. Somehow, Mercy had found a crack in his shored-up walls, and he very much feared she would keep pounding on them until she found a way in.

And God help him then.

***

'Sir, it's too late to visit *the Sail Loft* this evening. We have about three hours of daylight left. I don't think it's safe for us to be here once it gets dark. And we don't know how long it will take us to get there.' Percy was unusually insistent, and the Reverend hovered uncertainly.

'The fellow said it was in the Tobacco Dock – that's likely only fifteen minutes' walk from here,' the clergyman asserted, reluctant to abandon the search. 'We're close, Percy lad, I just know it.' He pursed his lips, looking this way and that as though the lodging house would suddenly materialise. 'I'll tell you what,' he proposed at length, 'we'll just *find* the place. I swear we won't go in - we'll leave that until tomorrow. And as soon as we get back, I'll send a note to Harding and ask him to come with us first thing. But think how much time we'll save if we can take him straight to it.'

Reluctantly, Percy acquiesced, and they began walking in the direction the barman had specified.

As they walked, Finn trailed behind them with Flossy. The boy made no bones about his disappointment over the lack of pickled eggs in the establishment they'd just left, sadly pronouncing himself fair *stairvin* in a voice that would have pulled at the heartstrings of the most hardened criminal.

Both the Reverend and Percy, entirely accustomed to the boy's incessant chatter, were paying no attention to his grumbles, busy watching for anything with a sign including the word *Sail*. Eventually, they broke free of the hodge podge of buildings, entering an open area that looked as though it had only recently been cleared. The Reverend guessed it had most likely been due to a fire since the ground was still blackened in places.

'How much further do you want to go, Sir,' Percy asked as they passed the makeshift shops and stalls that had sprung up in place of whatever had been there.

The Reverend sighed, admitting defeat. 'We must be getting close to the Tobacco Dock, but you're right Percy lad, time's getting on. We'll just have a quick look at that building over there, then we'll turn back.'

The two men continued on, Finn trailing behind them still grumbling, but just as they could see that the building they were making for actually might be a lodging house, a sudden panicked shout from Finn got their attention.

'*Flossy!*'

Startled, the two men watched as the little dog tore past them, dashing along the wharf before turning left onto the next jetty with Finn in hot pursuit, Flossy's collar and lead dangling in his hand.

'*Finn, stop,*' Percy yelled, lifting his cassock and giving chase.

'Thunder an' turf,' the Reverend muttered, picking up his own robe and hurrying after them. Turning onto the jetty, he bellowed, '*Flossy, stop right now if you don't want to end up in some Jack Tar's deuced pot.*'

The quay seemed to go forever, and Flossy didn't appear to have any intention of stopping. What the devil was she after?'

And then she disappeared.

By the time Reverend Shackleford arrived, winded and gasping, the little dog was nowhere to be seen.

***

Mercy did not enjoy the opera, and on her previous seasons had always feigned a megrim or some other minor ailment to avoid having to sit through one. This time though, she was actually looking forward to it. Or rather she was looking forward to seeing Nate.

She'd wondered whether she would be embarrassed to face him again after the unexpected consequences of throwing herself at him in the garden. But the truth was, if the opportunity presented itself, she'd do the same thing again – though perhaps not quite so forcefully…

She gave a small chuckle as she climbed down from the carriage outside the King's Theatre. This evening, Nate was meeting them in the foyer, though with the crush of people, she wondered if he'd even be able to find them. Holding onto her father's arm, she stepped into the sumptuous, brightly lit lobby, filled to bursting members of the *ton*, all dressed in their glittering best.

Given that several London theatres had already burned down due to the sheer number of candles alight, Mercy couldn't help eying the dripping chandeliers above the crowded reception area a little anxiously. Surely it wasn't necessary to have so many while it remained light outside?

Putting her concerns aside, she looked round for Nate, finally spotting him at the other side of the room conversing with her Aunt Patience and Uncle Max. She couldn't quite hide her surprise. To Mercy's knowledge, her aunt hated the opera with a passion. Then she grinned. Clearly it was Patience and Max's turn to babysit. She wished she'd been a fly on the roof of their carriage on the way here.

Wedged in between her father and stepmother, Mercedes fought her way over, noting with a thrill the exact moment Nate caught sight of her.

Her stomach did a little flip, and she felt a moment of true happiness. Then, seconds later, everything went to hell in a handcart.

Chapter Nineteen

Mercy's first indication that something wasn't quite right, was a slight tug on her reticule. Thinking she'd become tangled up with someone, she looked down, only to see a hand clamp itself tightly across her wrist. Heart constricting in sudden fear, she lifted her eyes to see who was on the other end of the almost skeletal fingers holding her in a death grip.

It was a man. She had time to notice he was well dressed before the crush of people around them hid him from her. Nevertheless, he didn't let go of her wrist, despite Mercy's frantic tugging. She shouted to her father, but the noise surrounding them was such that he continued on without realising she was no longer with him. She looked behind for her stepmother, but Chastity had been driven to one side in the crush.

Mercy realised she was being inexorably pulled to one side. Instinctively, her eyes sought Nate, and seconds later she found him. Although her abductor was blocked from his sight, he immediately picked up on the desperation in her face. With a barked comment to Max, he began to force his way towards her.

For a moment, Mercy thought she was safe, then she felt a prod in her side and with a sick feeling, realised whoever it was had a pistol. Any opportunity she'd had to scream for help was gone.

'There is another pistol trained on the Earl. If you value your father's life, you'll come with me without any fuss.'

Mercy tried to look behind her, wanting to see her abductor's face again, but the weapon dug painfully into her side as she did so. Not knowing what else to do, she allowed the man to pull her through the crush. He'd clearly chosen his moment well. There were so many people crammed into the room, that no one would notice as she was dragged outside. Tears formed in the corner of her eyes as she watched Nate trying to reach her. He wasn't going to get to her in time. She knew it and he knew it.

To her surprise, as her captor got closer to the outside doors, he suddenly changed his path. Linking his arm in hers, he marched her towards a previously unnoticed alcove.

Looking back, her frantic gaze locked on Nate's. Just before he disappeared from sight, she mouthed, 'I love you.' Whatever happened now, she couldn't bear it if he never knew how she felt.

***

As Nate frantically pushed his way through the throng, he had a clear view of Mercy being forcibly taken into an alcove close to the theatre entrance. He wanted to shout but had realised almost immediately that she had a gun pressed into her side. He dared not risk the bastard pressing the trigger. He guessed that the Earl wasn't yet aware his daughter had been abducted, but that was the least of his concerns.

Nate needed to get to her before she was bundled into a carriage and taken God knew where. By now, there was an undercurrent of disapproval following him. The unforgiveable rudeness of Viscount Carlingford would doubtless be discussed in every drawing room on the morrow.

Rudeness he could live with – anything, as long as they weren't gossiping about Mercy's abduction…

Ruthlessly he forged a path through bewildered bystanders, watching helplessly as she disappeared into the alcove. Clearly there was a door inside not generally used by the public. His heart slammed against his ribs at the thought that even now she might be lost to him.

A moment later, he finally broke free of the throng and hastened into the shadowy aperture. Predictably, the door was shut. With a quick look behind him to ensure Max and Christian had noted his direction, he pulled the door open and rushed inside.

The corridor was dark, winding to the right, but moments later, he was pushing open a second door to a narrow alley – just in time to see Mercy being forced into a waiting carriage. Adrenaline spiking, Nate raced towards the carriage, managing to jump onto the footplate just as the door was slammed and the coach driver snapped the reins to get the horses moving.

Hanging on for dear life, as the carriage careered round the corner, the Viscount grabbed hold of the handle, trying to force open the door. For a brief moment, he thought he might be successful, until the window was suddenly forced down and a pistol pointed directly at him.

Seconds later, there was a bang, followed by a sharp pain, and then nothing...

***

Augustus Shackleford couldn't remember the last time he was so distraught. Well, that wasn't quite true, it was when Freddy breathed his last. He hadn't been ready then, and he certainly wasn't deuced well ready now.

The three of them had spent the last hour and a half scouring the jetty, but the little dog appeared to have simply vanished. There was no sign of her in the water, though on more than one occasion they'd had to forcibly stop Finn from throwing himself in after a piece of flotsam he'd mistaken for Flossy.

If the Reverend was distressed, the boy was almost hysterical.

Even as the sun began to lower, Finn refused to leave the jetty, and in the end, the only way they managed to persuade him to go was to promise they'd resume looking at first light.

There were only three ships moored alongside the jetty, and the one nearest to where Flossy had disappeared was ironically flying an American flag. For a while Reverend Shackleford had even considered that she might be hiding on board, having somehow led them to Reinhardt. But when the sailor on watch had insisted no bloody animal had come aboard, the clergyman realised he was clutching at straws - attributing a human intelligence to an animal. Flossy was a clever madam, but she was still a deuced dog. And she'd only met the American once.

As much as it made him sick to the stomach to admit it, the most likely scenario was that she'd somehow fallen into the water and drowned.

As the three of them began the long trudge back towards the wharf. Percy had his arm around a weeping Finn. The boy was almost incoherent as they walked. Sobbing that it had been all been his fault, and he'd never eat another pickled egg as long as he lived. The curate had never felt so helpless in his life and found himself praying under his breath that they'd somehow find Flossy alive and well in the morning. He didn't think the boy would get any sleep this night.

Eventually they reached the place where Flossy had first run off, and the Reverend wondered for the first time whether the carriage driver would still be waiting for them by the time they got back to the Dock entrance. He knew that Christian and Chastity had been intending to take Mercy to the opera, so unless the coach driver had returned to the house and reported them missing, his daughter and son-in-law would be entirely unaware of any problem. They were both well accustomed to his foibles, and the fact that he and Percy hadn't joined them for dinner would be of no concern. He glanced down at his pocket watch.

Most likely they'd have left the house by now.

Sighing, Reverend Shackleford looked back the way they'd come, then forward in the direction they'd been headed. The building they'd been about to investigate was indeed a lodging house and the clergyman was wondering if they should even consider getting a room, just as a carriage came racing down the wharf.

'Tare an' hounds,' the Reverend breathed, hurriedly jumping out the way. 'What the devil is the world coming to when even a deuced coach driver's foxed.' He stepped in front of a shed - housing some kind of spice he guessed from the pungent smell - intending to walk round the back of it and cut behind the carriage, when all of a sudden, the carriage door crashed open revealing a young woman in evening dress. All three of them watched in surprise as the woman jumped down and took off in the direction they just come from. A second later, two men jumped down and chased after her. Predictably they caught up with her after a few minutes, and each grabbing an arm, marched her back towards the carriage.

The Reverend frowned. There were still plenty of people around, and none of the owners of the makeshift stalls had taken the slightest notice of the woman's plight, even though she was clearly being restrained against her will - even screaming to them for help. The clergyman stepped away from the shed, intending to ask what the devil they thought they were doing, when he saw a third man step down from the carriage.

It was Reinhardt.

Heart thumping, Augustus Shackleford instinctively stepped back out of sight, holding up his hand to Percy who looked as though he too was about to intervene.

As the woman came back into the clergyman's line of vision, he stifled a horrified gasp. Unbelievably, it was Mercy.

For once in his life, the Reverend had no idea what to do next. He could tell that the thug dragging her was carrying a pistol. If he and Percy tried to intervene, they could very well end up going for an impromptu swim, and that wouldn't help anyone, least of all his granddaughter. He glanced over at his curate's shocked face. Clearly Percy had recognised her too.

Helplessly, they watched as she was taken towards the lodging house. They didn't enter through the front door, instead dragging Mercy into an alley at the side. The Reverend felt panic welling up. Did they intend to murder her?

Then common sense kicked in. Of course, the varmint wouldn't risk such a thing in broad daylight. It was one thing to hold a woman against her will – sadly such things were commonplace – but murder? Murder he could hang for. And Reinhardt needed Mercy alive.

As if to clarify his intention, the Reverend faintly heard Reinhardt ask his cohort if the priest was on his way, just before they disappeared round the back of the building.

So, he didn't have a priest ready and waiting upstairs to conduct the ceremony... Reverend Shackleford thought back to the ship they'd just seen with the American flag. That was likely the vessel Reinhardt intended to escape on once he'd made Mercy his legal property, but the villain hadn't done it yet.

The clergyman took a deep breath then gritted his teeth. There was no time to fetch anyone else. It was up to him, Percy and the Almighty now. He turned towards his white-faced curate and suddenly spotted Finn, sitting with his back against the shed. For a few minutes, he'd forgotten the boy was with them. Staring at the lad's tear-stained face, the Reverend suddenly had an idea...

***

As Nate lay on the ground, he briefly wondered if he was dying. His right arm hurt like the devil and, for a second, he couldn't remember what the hell he was doing there.

Seconds later it all came flooding back. Lifting his head, he saw that the carriage was nowhere to be seen. The bastard had Mercy. Groaning he rolled to his left side and pushed himself up to a sitting position before beginning the laborious task of shrugging off his jacket. Once down to his shirt, he inspected his right arm.

His shirt was soaked in blood, but though the wound was still bleeding profusely, the bullet looked to have gone right through the fleshy part of his arm. He picked up his discarded jacket and was staunching the wound with it when shouts heralded the arrival of Christian and Max.

Nate pointed in the direction the carriage had taken. 'I'm fine, it's only a flesh wound. Go.'

The two men ran to the mouth of the alley and disappeared leaving Nate to struggle to his feet. The Viscount hoped to God the carriage was trapped in the queue surrounding the Haymarket. Leaning against the wall, he closed his eyes, waiting for the sudden faintness to pass. Then tugging at the cravat around his neck, he used the cloth as a makeshift tourniquet, wrapping it tightly around his arm and tying it off with his teeth.

Pushing away from the wall, he staggered back to the alleyway entrance, looking in the direction the carriage had taken. His heart sank as he realised the lane didn't come out at the front of the theatre, but the back. His bearings had got completely skewed in the twisting corridor. Here, all was quiet with only the distant buzz of conversation coming from inside the theatre. Holding onto a lamp post, he watched and waited for Christian and Max's return, knowing in his heart of hearts they would not have been in time to stop Reinhardt.

Moments later the door opened behind him, and he turned to see

Chastity and Patience hurrying towards him.

'How badly are you hurt?' Patience asked without preamble.

'A flesh wound,' the Viscount answered shortly. 'Reinhardt has Mercy. Christian and Max have gone after the carriage.'

Chastity gave a low moan, covering her mouth with her hand.

Patience was more pragmatic. 'It needs cleaning,' she announced, 'and for that we need to get you inside. It might only be a flesh wound, but if putrefaction sets in, it'll be curtains for you all the same, my lord.'

At that moment, Christian and Max appeared round the corner. The despondent looks on their faces clearly revealed their failure to stop the carriage.

'There was no sign of it,' Max grimaced.

'Did you see which way it went once it reached the end of the street?' Christian growled.

Nate shook his head. 'The shot propelled me off the foot plate and I think I blacked out for a second.'

Christian ran his fingers through his hair in weary anxiety. 'Forgive my abruptness. How bad is your injury?'

'Bad enough,' interjected Patience. 'He certainly can't go rushing off anywhere before it's properly cleaned and dressed.'

'Did you catch sight of the carriage at all?' Nate asked, gritting his teeth at the thought that in a few hours Mercy might be beyond any help they could give.

Max shrugged. 'We saw plenty of carriages, but there was no way of knowing whether any of them had Mercy inside.' He grimaced. 'Clearly the driver knew his way around the warren of backstreets. They could be anywhere now.'

Nate frowned and shook his head, suddenly recalling the strange smell emanating from the opened window. 'Not anywhere,' he mused, trying to place the pungent smell he remembered. 'Spices,' he said at length. 'Specifically, *cloves.*' He paused, thinking back to the hand holding the gun. 'I don't think the man who shot me was Reinhardt. The hand was none too clean, and the arm of his jacket was stained and torn. But underneath the reek of stale sweat, was the smell of cloves.'

He looked over at Christian, suddenly animated. 'Why would a varmint like that smell of cloves? It was all over his fingers.'

'The docks,' Max and Christian said at the same time. Nate nodded slowly.

'It makes sense. Reinhardt will want to be close to whatever ship he's booked passage on. There are lots of inns and taverns around the docks he could hole up in while waiting to set sail....' He paused and Christian continued.

'So, wherever he's staying might be close to a warehouse storing cloves. Is it possible that the man who shot you is a dock worker?'

'More likely a gallows bird who saw an opportunity to make a quick profit,' Max countered. 'Reinhardt probably had the lodging ready and waiting for a quick getaway.'

'Doesn't he need to wed Mercy first?' Patience asked.

'He could quite easily do that in a tavern bedchamber,' Max returned. 'He's probably had some soused priest on standby for a while. There are many less than scrupulous so-called servants of God who'll do anything for their next bottle of communion wine.'

'It's a bit tenuous,' Patience muttered, shaking her head.

'You're right love, it is - but it's all we've got,' Max retorted with a grimace.

Chastity gripped her husband's arm. 'You can't go into the Docklands alone,' she declared firmly. 'We have to contact Jamie. He'll be able to provide the men you need to assist you.'

Christian nodded. 'But we dare not wait for him to muster his Runners. In the meantime, we need Adam and Gabriel.' He looked down at his wife. 'You and Patience take our carriage to Jamie and Prudence.'

He looked at the Viscount, who even in the dim light was beginning to resemble a corpse. 'You too, Nate. Prudence will have the necessary materials to clean and dress the wound.'

Patience snorted. 'As long as she doesn't do the actual dressing. I doubt the Viscount will last the night after being ministered to by Pru.'

When Nate frowned and opened his mouth to protest, the Earl held up his hand. 'You're no use to me in this state, Harding,' he ground out. 'We both know it. Get the wound dressed. You can fill Jamie in and join us once you've stopped damn well leaking.' He turned to Max.

'We'll take your carriage. Adam's house is the closest, I think. While we wait for him to dress, we can send a messenger to Gabe. Hopefully he'll be ready for us by the time we get to him. With luck, we'll be in the Docks well before dark.'

Chapter Twenty

Mercy had never been so terrified in her entire life. But it wasn't for herself. The moment she heard the shot and saw Nate fall from the carriage would live with her forever. All she could think about was the sight of his body lying on the cobbles. His black evening dress had prevented her from seeing exactly where he'd been shot so she had no way of knowing whether he was dead or alive.

She looked at Reinhardt's cold, impassive face and wanted to spit in it. It was the first time she'd actually seen him in the flesh and his hand on her arm made her skin crawl. As if in answer to her silent hatred, his grip tightened painfully on her arm.

There were two other men in the carriage with them – both clearly thugs for hire.

'I don't reckon I did more 'an wing 'im,' the one with the gun said, shoving the pistol down his stained britches.

'Well, you din't get off two shots, Davy, so I'd watch where you put that if I wos you,' the other man chortled, 'Wi' your aim, you'll just as likely shoot yer baubles off – mind you, at least you won't need to worry 'bout meetin' ol' Derrick.'

'If I swing, I'll bloody take you wi' me, Smiffy.' Clearly there was no love lost between the two men.

Biting her lip, Mercy looked down at her lap. She needed to get a grip on her fear. She had to put Nate out of her mind. If the wretch was right, he'd only been wounded, not killed. She took a deep breath, trying to calm her nerves. Watch, listen and take the first opportunity to run. That was the only way she'd get out of this.

She raised her head and looked out of the window. At first, she didn't recognise where they were, but after a few minutes she realised they were heading for London Docks. A fresh surge of fear engulfed her. Obviously, Reinhardt intended to wed her, then board the first ship back to America.

But why did he want her so badly? Mercy had no illusions about herself. She was pretty, certainly, but hardly a diamond of the first water - and to come all the way from America... She glowered down at her knees. Likely her father was right – it was something to do with her mother. She sneaked a brief glance at her captor. Did she dare try and find out what? If she simply asked him, would he tell her? Then she berated herself. Now was not the time to find out what the blackguard wanted - He'd no doubt give it to her chapter and verse after they were leg shackled. She needed to be out of his clutches before that happened.

She looked back out of the window. Though Reinhardt still had hold of her arm, he'd relaxed his grip slightly. Nobody spoke and the atmosphere in the carriage was one of tense anticipation. Did he intend to wed her this night? She shoved down the sheer terror at the thought of what might follow after. The thought of sharing her captor's bed made her feel physically sick.

Mercy became aware that they'd entered the Dockyard as the carriage took a sharp right, running alongside the wharfs. She took heart from the number of people still milling around the quayside, but then she realised that even though it was still relatively early in the evening, quite a few of them were Haymarket ware. If she cried for help, she'd be unlikely to receive it from that direction.

Biting her lip again, she did her best to memorise her surroundings, but gradually realised that all the wharfs looked the same. They passed warehouse after warehouse interspersed with pubs, lodging houses and pawnbrokers. Plenty of venders were still abroad peddling their goods – mostly foodstuffs by the look of things. If she appealed to any of them for assistance, would they give it? Surely there were dock police patrolling the area. Mayhap she could persuade one of them to run for help.

Mercy's mind went in increasingly desperate circles as she sought a way out of her predicament, until finally she felt, rather than saw the carriage slowing down. Her heart gave a dull thud as she attempted to see where they were.

Both henchmen shifted slightly, clearly getting ready to climb out of the carriage first. Mercy stiffened, then tried to relax, swallowing her increasing panic. She subtly shifted away from her captor, and to her surprise, he didn't react, seemingly preoccupied by their arrival.

Heart slamming against her ribs, she tensed, getting ready to move as soon as the carriage stopped. Glancing over at Reinhardt she saw he was looking through the other window and with a thrill of terror, realised they were approaching a lodging house. It was now or never.

Without waiting for the carriage to come to a full stop, she leapt to her feet, grabbing hold of the door handle at the same time. Evidently not expecting her to make a run for it, Reinhardt hadn't maintained a tight grip on her arm, and she was able to yank it free as she thrust open the door and leapt down. As soon as she landed, she picked up her skirts, kicked off her evening pumps, and ran.

She'd hoped to be able to lose herself in the myriad of alleys surrounding the buildings to the left, but to her horror, they'd stopped close to a wide-open area that looked as though it had recently been cleared after a fire. Swearing under her breath, she sobbed her frustration, hearing the unmistakable sound of her pursuers gaining on her. She wasn't going to make it. There was an almost village sized collection of makeshift shops and stalls inside the open area, and turning towards them, she screamed for help.

To her horror, she was totally ignored. No one, absolutely *no one* came to her aid – not even challenging the two thugs who took hold of her arms none too gently.

Mercedes sobbed softly as she was led back to her captor who was now regarding her like she was something less than human.

All fight had gone out of her and she let them pull her towards the lodging house. To her surprise, they didn't take her through the front door, but into a narrow passageway to the side. White hot fear had her briefly fighting against the arms that held her, but a sudden back-handed slap across her face shocked her into silence.

Seconds later she was dragged through a door and up a narrow set of stairs into a room that actually resembled the bedchamber she'd been given in Carlingford Hall. She swallowed a sudden hysterical laugh, half expecting a priest to suddenly crawl out from under the bed.

'Tie her to the chair.' The order was given almost indifferently, in complete contrast to the slap he'd dealt her minutes earlier.

Mercy battled her panic as they forced her down into a chair, trussing her up like a chicken. Despite her fear that they'd do something terrible while she was tied up and helpless, she was completely ignored, and as the minutes ticked by, she realised they were waiting for the priest to arrive.

'A man of God is unlikely to marry us while I'm bound to a chair,' she said at length. Mercy knew her comment was unwise, but she was desperate to find out if there was any chance of appealing the priest's conscience.

All three laughed and her last hope withered and died. 'You reckon 'e's goin' ter refuse to do the deed since yer bride don't look none too 'appy about it?' The man named Davy slapped his thigh in delight.

'I object,' Smith parodied in a high voice.

Mercy blinked furiously. Whatever happened she would not cry in front of these... animals.

Seconds later, footsteps sounded up the stairs.

'that'll be 'is revrenship now – shall we ask 'im?

'*Enough!*' Reinhardt's command was imperious but without emotion, until abruptly he gave the most malevolent grin Mercy had ever seen. Her heart constricted in terror as he added, 'Show some respect, gentlemen. Today is my wedding day...'

***

Within an hour of Mercy's abduction, Christian, Max, Adam and Gabriel were on their way to London Docks. Although all four were thinking it, none of them voiced the concern that they could be chasing a red herring.

If Mercy wasn't being held in the Docks, they had no idea where she could possibly be. And if that proved to be the case, all four men were painfully aware she was lost.

The mood in the carriage was tense. All of them were carrying pistols they wouldn't hesitate to use should the need arise. Their plan was vague at best. If Reinhardt was holding Mercy in the Dockyard, it would likely be somewhere he'd already picked out, as Max suggested. If that proved to be the case, the American must have spent at least some time going backwards and forwards to the lodgings.

Surely someone would have seen him.

Of course, Reinhardt might have been staying in the Docks for the whole of his time in London, but all four men agreed it was unlikely. His lodging in the Dockyards would be near to the ship he'd bought passage on, and he wouldn't have risked staying so close until he knew his plan was about to come to fruition.

As they approached the entrance to the Eastern Docks, Christian was surprised to see one of his carriages waiting at the side of the road. Frowning at the others, he climbed down and hurried over to the coach driver to ask what the devil he thought he was doing.

Minutes later, he came back, his face grim. 'We have another problem. It seems that Augustus, Percy and Finn are inside the Dockyard somewhere. They were dropped off just before three when the Reverend requested they be collected around five.

'Unfortunately, the coach driver hasn't seen them since.'

***

Nate gritted his teeth as his arm was soaked in liqueur for the second time in as many minutes. It seemed that Prudence and Patience could not agree on the amount of alcohol necessary to disinfect the wound. Prudence favoured the 'the more alcoholic the better,' method, whilst Patience simply poured on whatever she could lay her hands on. Either way, the Viscount suspected that if any self-respecting infection was even considering settling in his arm, the half bottle of blue ruin currently soaking into his veins would very likely have put paid to the idea.

Unfortunately, both sisters agreed that the wound needed stitching, but at that point Chastity had stepped in. Apparently, she'd always been the *seamstress* of the family. And looking at his arm nearly an hour after the bullet had gone through it, Nate was simply glad it hadn't had to be amputated.

While the sisters were ministering to his wound, Nate had updated Jamie on the events of the evening and the magistrate was already in the process of gathering together a number of Runners to search the Docks – focusing on those wharfs specialising in spices.

'Father actually spoke with me earlier today asking about ships to the Americas,' Prudence commented thoughtfully, handing a roll of cloth to Chastity. 'I told him I'd speak with our cook who has a nephew working in the Docks. Mrs. Shearing hasn't reported back to me yet, but I'll go and speak with her now to find out if she's heard anything.'

'It might have been helpful if you'd remembered that earlier,' snapped Patience, 'since all our husbands could well be on a wild goose chase.'

Prudence reddened. 'It slipped my mind with Mr. Harding's injury and all the talk of lodging houses and spices,' she retorted defensively. 'I'll go and speak with her now.'

As she hurried from the room, Chastity frowned at Patience. 'Was it necessary to be quite so scathing?' she scolded, stabbing her unfortunate patient with the needle to emphasise her point.

Nate winced and hurriedly intervened before a full-blown argument could erupt. His wound already hurt like the blazes, and he'd be of no use to Mercy at all after being her stepmother's pin cushion. Hopefully Christian will catch Reinhardt before he forces Mercy to wed him,' he commented through gritted teeth.

'What will happen if he fails to find her before then and the marriage has taken place?' Chastity asked fearfully, giving him another stab.

'From a legal standpoint, providing all the paperwork is in order, there's very little any of us can do,' Patience answered with a sigh.

'Except make her a widow,' Nate countered grimly.

At that moment, Prudence reappeared. 'Anything?' Patience asked, her tone much more conciliatory.

Prudence gave an agitated nod. 'Apparently there's a ship named the *Western Star* moored alongside in the Tobacco Dock that's due to sail imminently – mayhap on the next tide.'

Nate swore softly. 'That's why Reinhardt's acted so hastily – he's hoping we won't have time to stop him.' He turned to Prudence as Chastity finished wrapping his arm. 'Can you send someone with a message to my house?' he asked her. 'Tell the groom to saddle Duchess and have her and Ruby brought here as soon as possible.'

'What are you going to do?' Patience asked.

'There are enough men searching for the lodging house. If I head straight for the *Western Star*, I'll make certain Reinhardt doesn't leave the country.' He climbed to his feet, wincing as he accidentally flexed his arm.

'Horseback riding will likely open your wound,' Patience advised caustically.

'Not if I ride Duchess. She's battle trained and will react to my leg movements.' Nate explained.

'And who's Ruby.'

'His dog.'

'Is she battle trained too?'

Nate gave a fierce grin. 'No, but she's a first-class ratter.'

***

After ushering Percy behind the spice shed, Reverend Shackleford asked him when he'd last married anybody.

Percy gave him a puzzled look. 'I've only done it the once, Sir. You married Lizzy and me yourself.'

The Reverend stared at him for a second, then sighed. 'Sometimes Percy, I swear the Almighty has the strangest sense of humour. I'm not talking about you and Lizzy. When was the last time you conducted a marriage ceremony?'

Percy frowned. 'May Day,' he answered promptly. 'Just before Finn and I left for London. Bit of an urgent affair as I remember since the baby was well overdue.'

Reverend Shackleford sighed again. 'David and Dolly, I take it. I told old man Parsons he couldn't expect the lad to keep his hands to himself if he insisted on spending every night in the Red Lion while he left 'em to their own devices.'

'I think Mr. Parsons was secretly pleased in truth,' Percy retorted. 'He looked very happy at the wedding.'

The Reverend nodded. 'I can understand that. If I remember rightly, Dolly Parsons has a face like a bag of broken crabs.' He shook his head, then waved his hand in dismissal. 'Anyway, now's not the time to discuss the love lives of the residents of Blackmore. Could you repeat the ceremony word for word if you had to?'

Percy creased his brow. 'I think so, Sir. Why do you ask?'

'You're going to conduct Mercy and that blackguard Reinhardt's wedding.'

The curate stared at his superior in horror. 'I couldn't possibly do that, Sir. I'd never forgive myself.'

The Reverend groaned in frustration. 'I'm not asking you to conduct a *proper* ceremony,' he retorted in exasperation. 'Nothing legal, anyway. That's why I wanted to know if you remembered it word for word. It's easy to get the crucial bits wrong, if you know what they should be.'

'But what about the real vicar?' Percy insisted, 'and why can't you do it?'

'The real one's not here yet. And if I go up there, Reinhardt will recognise me.

'So, what are you going to do?'

The Reverend opened his mouth and shut it again. This was the part of the plan he'd not finalised yet. If Flossy had been here, he'd have used her as the distraction. He swallowed a sudden urge to break down and cry.

'Finn will provide a disturbance,' the clergyman declared gruffly, 'once you've started your *dearly beloved* bit.'

The curate looked at his superior in dismay. 'Lizzy'll have my baubles,' he gulped.

'Dinni fash yersel, Da,' Finn piped up climbing to his feet. The lad dashed the remaining tears from his eyes. 'It's up tae us tae stop the bastard.' He didn't apologise for his language and neither man berated him as he sniffed and added, 'Ah ken it be what Flossy'd want.'

Chapter Twenty-One

Max gave a fatalistic shrug at this latest turn of events. 'In my experience, Augustus is more than capable of looking after himself. Our priority has to be Mercy.'

Christian nodded. 'I told the coachman to stay where he is. Hopefully the Reverend will turn up eventually, though I'd feel a lot happier if he and Percy didn't have the lad with them.'

'They took Finn?' Adam exclaimed shaking his head in disbelief. 'That puts a different spin on things.'

'Well, I've no doubt Augustus is here for the same thing we are,' Gabriel commented drily, 'so if we find Mercy, we'll doubtless run into the Reverend at the same time.' He shook his head at the idiosyncrasies of his father-in-law.

'The Dock Master's office is close, so I'll go and speak with him,' Christian continued. 'If he can tell us where any warehouses storing cloves are situated it'll save us tearing the whole Dockyard apart.'

'While we're waiting, I propose we ask around to find out if anybody hereabout saw Reinhardt's carriage,' Max suggested. 'It couldn't have been much more than an hour ago.'

'You might be wise to warn the Dock Master that Jamie's on his way with a contingent of Runners,' Adam advised as all four climbed out of the carriage. 'The new police force here won't be happy about having their toes trodden on.'

Christian gave a rueful nod. 'The last thing we need is a fight between two bloody law enforcement agencies.' He looked down at his watch. 'I suggest we reconvene here in fifteen minutes.'

As Christian strode away, the other three split up to ask those in the vicinity if anyone had seen a carriage carrying three men and a young woman. Predictably no one had seen or heard anything. By the time Christian returned, they were already back in the carriage waiting impatiently.

'The largest clove warehouse is in the Western Dock, wharf sixteen,' the Earl announced as he climbed into the carriage. 'We'll get there quicker if we go in via the western entrance.' The carriage was already moving as he sat down.

'Did he say if there were any lodging houses close by?' Gabriel asked.

'Several,' Christian answered shortly. 'I take it no one saw Reinhardt's carriage.' He gave a humourless laugh.

'Not even for the blunt,' Adam growled.

'They live in a world where it's unhealthy to see or hear anything except their own arses,' Max sighed.

Christian nodded, swallowing an urge to punch something. They were running out of time. He could feel it. How long would it take them to search all the lodging houses close to the warehouse? It was like looking for a bloody needle in a haystack when they didn't even know if they were in the right field.

***

Mercy watched the door in almost hypnotic fascination as the footsteps stopped just outside. Seconds later there was a timid knock.

'Well, answer the bloody thing,' Reinhardt snarled when his two henchmen didn't move.

They both immediately hurried to the door, jostling each other to get there first. In the end, Smith grabbed hold of the latch first and wrenched the door open.

For a second the two men blocked her view, but as one of them shifted and said, 'Who the bloody 'ell are you?' it took all of Mercy's control to keep a blank face as she recognised Percy Noon standing on the landing.

'Where's Evans,' Reinhardt growled, stepping forward threateningly. He pulled his pistol out of his jacket pocket. Mercy stifled a gasp of fear.

'He's sick,' Percy responded weakly. Mercedes knew the curate wasn't feigning his trembling. 'I… I think it was some bad meat.'

'Drank himself into a bloody stupor you mean,' Reinhardt ground out, his anger palpable.

'I can conduct the ceremony,' Percy continued, his voice getting stronger. 'But I want the fee you promised Evans.'

'Did the idiot send you?' Reinhardt spat out. 'How do I know you're not cutting a wheedle?'

Percy was getting into his stride. 'I can quote the marriage service by heart,' he answered boldly.

Reinhardt visibly wavered, then he pointed his pistol towards Mercy. 'Get on with it then,' he finally said between gritted teeth.

Percy gave a quick glance towards her as he rummaged in his cassock, eventually pulling out a dog-eared Bible. 'May I ask the young lady's name?' he asked at length with a small cough.

'Mercedes Stanhope.' Reinhardt snapped the words.

'Err, will she be able to stand for her vows?' Percy queried.

The American swore softly. 'Untie her,' he ordered.

Seconds later, Mercy was rubbing her wrists as she got slowly to her feet.

'Please stand closer to your... husband to be,' the curate ordered. Mercy was pushed roughly towards Reinhardt, who grabbed hold of her arm, pulling her against him.

'Dearly beloved,' Percy began, glancing behind her to the window.

Reinhardt didn't appear to notice, but Mercy had to resist the urge to look behind her. Seconds later there was a loud crash.

'*Ah'll nae be giein ye ma purse ye tumshie, so gaun jus' bugger aff wid ye. HELP, HELP.*'

Incredibly, Mercy realised the voice was Finn's and it was coming from underneath the window. She'd had no idea he could shout so loudly.

'Ignore it,' ordered Reinhardt through gritted teeth.

'*Ech, he be awa in the heid. HELP. Ah'm bein KILL'D.*'

'I'm afraid I'm unable to continue with such a racket going on outside,' Percy said diffidently. 'Perhaps one of your associates might encourage the person to stop?'

HELP. Ah'm gaun tae be *DEID.*'

'For God's sake, get down there and shut the little bastard up. I don't care how you do it.'

Smith wrenched open the door and clattered down the stairs. 'Shut the bloody door,' Reinhardt ground out as the yells got suddenly louder.

Glancing at Mercy, Percy obligingly went over to the door, but before he could shut it there was a loud clang and for a second the yelling stopped.

'Thank G...' Reinhardt began, then

'Ah'm bein MURDER'D. HELP.'

'Find out what the hell the idiot's doing.' Reinhardt was nearly incandescent with rage as his second ruffian took to the stairs. Waving his pistol towards Percy he bit out, 'Get. On. With. It.'

'Dearly beloved,' Percy started again. There was a second clang, followed by silence.

'Dearly beloved,' he repeated, only to be stopped this time as Reinhardt suddenly held up his hand. 'Is something wrong?' the curate asked timidly.

'Where the hell are they?' He let go of Mercy's arm and pushed her back towards the chair, 'Sit' he barked. Swallowing her fear, she sat down.

'They do know they are required as witnesses?' Percy's hesitant words were apologetic.

'I know they're required as witnesses,' Reinhardt shot back savagely. 'That's why they're here.'

The curate gave a small cough. 'Except they're not,' he pointed out politely.

By this time Reinhardt was waving his pistol around like he was conducting an orchestra and Mercy found herself shutting her eyes every time he directed it towards her.

She had no idea what her grandfather could possibly have done to shut the two thugs up and she could only hope that whatever it was didn't traumatise Finn forever. Not daring to move she watched as Reinhardt strode towards the window. While he was trying to see through the grimy glass, she tried to catch Percy's eye, but when the curate gave a small shrug, she realised with a surge of terror that he didn't know what the Reverend was up to either...

***

Nate managed to mount Duchess without too much trouble, though it had been a long time since the mare had been required to kneel onto her forelegs to help him. He took hold of the reins with his left hand and whistled to Ruby, who'd been enjoying all the extra attention.

Chastity took hold of Duchess's bridle. 'Take care, Nate,' she murmured. 'Don't do anything foolish unless it's to push Reinhardt into the Thames.'

Patience gave an inelegant snort. 'He might be able to swim. I say if you get the chance, shoot the bastard.' She paused, then frowned. 'You can shoot with your left hand I take it?'

'If you can't, you can always string him up,' Prudence suggested, her old spark returning.

Nate raised his eyebrows. Were all the sisters this bloodthirsty? He swiftly pulled the pistol from where it was tucked in his waistband, to demonstrate his effectiveness with his left hand, but all he said was, 'Trust me, whatever happens, he'll never come for her again.' Then, using his knees to wheel Duchess around he cantered out onto the street, Ruby at the mare's heels.

There were fewer carriages on the roads than there had been on the way to the opera and Nate slowed Duchess down to avoid her slipping on the hard cobbles. It was a long time since he'd been inside London Docks. The last time was on his return from Belgium, when those at Wapping were still very new.

To his surprise, very little had changed, and as he entered through the Eastern entrance, he slowed Duchess down to a walk. According to the information he'd been given, the *Western Star* was moored on one of the jetties in the small basin known as the Tobacco Dock that linked the Eastern and Western Docks. But exactly where, he had no idea. Likely he'd be able to get the information from the Dock Master, but given the sheer number of ships coming and going, it would be quicker to simply make his way straight along the wharf and look for himself.

Throughout the journey, Nate had ruthlessly forced his concern for Mercy aside, concentrating only on what he needed to do. But as he rode Duchess down the still busy wharf, he found it more and more difficult to stifle the fear that he'd be too late. That somehow, Reinhardt would already have set sail and claimed her as his own.

He'd told Mercedes that he didn't know how to love. But that wasn't quite true. He'd known in his heart of hearts that he'd loved Mercy since the moment she walked into the stables. But now, finally, he allowed himself to surrender to the all-powerful feelings she provoked in him.

If he didn't manage to save her, how the hell would he ever save himself?

**

'Right then, when I asked about rooms, the landlady said she's not taking any lodgers at the moment, so likely our American has the place to himself. Better still, when I asked her if she knew of any other establishments, she said she hadn't got time to stand and jaw since she was on her way out and wouldn't be back until later on this evening. So, it's all good for us as it means the place'll be empty apart from Reinhardt's room. Percy are you clear about your part of the plan?'

The curate swallowed and took a deep breath. 'I'm to go in through the front door and ask for the American...' He paused and frowned, 'How can I ask for him if there's no one there to ask?'

The Reverend sighed. 'Use what passes for your brain Percy. If there's no one there apart from Reinhardt, how difficult will it be to find out which room he's in? There can't be that many bedchambers, and we know his is on the back.'

The curate nodded uncertainly. 'Once I get to the room, I tell Reinhardt that the priest he had the arrangement with is sick and has sent me in his stead.'

'Well, you'll need to sound a bit more convincing than that.'

'What do I do if the real one turns up halfway through the ceremony?'

'Leave him to me and Finn,' Reverend Shackleford answered promptly.

Percy stared at the clergyman in horrified silence. 'What will you do with him? You can't involve Finn in anything so smoky.'

'Dinnae fash yersel, Da,' the boy said for the second time. 'The God botherer'll nae gie us any trouble.'

'You won't kill him?' Percy asked the Reverend fearfully.

'Of course I won't deuced well kill him,' Augustus Shackleford, retorted, shocked. 'Tare an' hounds, lad, what do you take me for? I'll just give him a deuced headache he won't forget. And you never know, mayhap it'll help bring the scoundrel back to the light.'

'So, what kind of disturbance do you have in mind, Sir?' the curate asked, only slightly mollified.

'Well, so far, I've in my head that Finn'll make a racket. Reinhardt's thugs will come down to investigate and I'll give 'em what for.'

Percy stared at his superior in silence, waiting for the rest of the details. The Reverend stared back.

After about a minute, the curate frowned. 'That's it?'

'It's all you need to know, Percy my boy.' The Reverend tapped his nose and winked. His other hand was behind his back with the fingers crossed. This was seriously getting to be a habit. The truth was, he didn't have anything more to tell the curate because he had no actual idea how he was going to give 'em *what for*.

Percy felt a familiar sense of dread swamp him, even more so when he looked over at Finn and saw the very same eagerness in his adopted son's face. He stifled a moan. Lizzy was going to string him up for this.

'Now then, I think it's best if you go and get yourself into position,' Reverend Shackleford continued, desperate to forestall any more awkward questions. 'As soon as we're ready, we'll give you a signal.'

'What signal?'

'Thunder an' turf, Percy, you don't need to know everything. Just watch for a deuced *signal*.'

'Where do you want me to wait?'

Augustus Shackleford gave a long-suffering sigh.

'Mebbe ye can hide roond the corner o' the lodging hoose?' Finn interrupted, earning him an approving nod from the Reverend. Percy felt his sense of doom increase to Biblical proportions as the clergyman ushered him round the back of the spice shed.

'I'll tell you as soon as the coast is clear,' Reverend Shackleford hissed, looking back towards the lodging house. 'Try not to look too suspicious.'

Minutes later it was just him and Finn. Once Percy had given them a reluctant thumbs up from his position at the side of the lodging house, the Reverend sank down onto the wooden planking.

'I'll be honest with you, lad,' the clergyman said after a few seconds. 'I haven't a deuced clue how we're going to stop

Reinhardt's thugs. If you've got any bright ideas, both the Almighty and I will be eternally grateful if you'd share 'em.'

Finn thought for a second. 'Dae ye hae onythin' at all tae gie 'em whit fer?'

'Not a thing,' the Reverend mourned.

Finn sat silently for a second, then abruptly scrambled to his feet. 'Dae ye hae any coin?' he asked, holding out his hand. Grumbling, the clergyman dug into his pockets and came up with a couple of shillings. 'Stay whare ye are,' Finn ordered, pocketing the money before tiptoeing all the way round the spice shed, clearly trying to avoid being spotted by an already distraught Percy.

Reverend Shackleford watched him dash across the wharf towards the open area containing the makeshift stalls. He actually felt quite emotional. Finn might be Percy's, but he was a boy after the Reverend's own heart.

Minutes later he came back with a large frying pan and held it out to the Reverend with a flourish.

Taking the pan Augustus Shackleford climbed to his feet, his enthusiasm entirely renewed. After swiping it this way and that, he patted the lad on the back. 'You're a chip off the old block and no mistake Finn Noon,' he declared with a grin. 'Come along, let's go and get the varmints.'

Waving his pan gaily at a panic-stricken Percy, the Reverend led Finn round the back of the lodging house. Once there, he looked around for something he could stand on. Fortunately, there was an old chair that appeared sturdy enough. Dragging it next to the back entrance door, the Reverend climbed up and tucked his cassock into his breeches. After a few seconds, he gave a thumbs up sign to Finn, who promptly ran round the side of the house and waved to Percy who was now so pale, he looked like a bad piece of taxidermy.

Seconds later the boy was back. 'We'll give your da enough time to get up there, and then we give 'em what for,' the clergyman announced gleefully.

While they waited, Reverend Shackleford gave the pan a few experimental swings, then looking down at his pocket watch, he finally gave a nod.

Seconds later, Finn's shout was loud enough to wake the dead.

It was only two minutes before they heard the clatter of feet down the stairs. Reverend Shackleford readied himself, legs bent like he was about to deliver a blistering tennis serve. As the door opened, he swung the pan to the side, and as soon as the varmint stepped through, brought it down in a smack that would have felled Goliath himself.

Chapter Twenty-Two

It took Nate another twenty minutes to find the *Western Star* and as soon as he'd identified the ship, he took Duchess to the nearest tavern, back along the wharf about a quarter of a mile. Fortunately, the establishment had a small, if crude, stable attached to the side.

Ignoring the mare's reproachful looks as he struggled to take off her saddle using one hand, Nate brushed her down as best he could and gave her some oats. He'd paid for a full night, with instructions that if he didn't return on the morrow, the innkeeper was to send word to the Countess of Cottesmore, who would arrange to have the horse collected.

Ruby, he trusted to find her own way home should she need to.

Once he was certain the mare was safe at least, Nate returned to the jetty on which the *Western Star* was moored. It was flying an American flag and the number of sailors running up and down the rigging gave every indication that her leaving was imminent. There was no hint as to whether Reinhardt was on board, but somehow Nate didn't think so. The bastard wouldn't have had time to get the marriage ceremony over with and would be unlikely to want to spend his wedding night in the same pokey cabin he was going to have to live in for the next couple of months.

Shoving down the rage that consumed him at the thought of

Reinhardt forcing Mercy into his bed, Nate looked back towards the wharf. There was a lodging house about another fifty yards along. Could that be where Reinhardt was holding Mercy?

There was no sign of Christian and the others. Surely, they should have been here by now. Had he got it wrong, or had they?

He stood for a moment, debating his next move, when all of a sudden Ruby gave an excited bark at his feet before dashing towards the *Star's* gangplank. Hurriedly, Nate started after her, worried the dog might take it into her head to run onto the deck. But as she reached the ropes tying the plank of wood to the jetty, Ruby simply stood, wagging her tail. Seconds later, to Nate's complete amazement the diminutive shape of Flossy appeared on the other end of the gangplank with something incongruously dangling from her mouth.

The Viscount glanced over to the nearest sailor, but he seemed oblivious to the little dog's presence.

Heart in his mouth, Nate called softly to her, crouching down in invitation and praying she wouldn't turn round and go back the way she'd come.

Instead, with every evidence of satisfaction, Flossy jumped onto the gangplank and ran towards Ruby. As she reached the terrier, the little dog dropped what she was carrying and rolled on to her back, clearly delighted to see her friend.

Nate hurried over to them and quickly scooped Flossy up with his good arm. He couldn't even begin to guess where the Reverend was, and a sudden sick feeling assailed him. Could the clergyman somehow be on board the ship? Keeping the little dog under his arm, he crouched down again to see what she'd dropped, wincing as he picked it up using his injured arm.

It was a tiny key, not even half an inch across, threaded onto a narrow satin ribbon. Clearly old, he couldn't imagine what it opened, or why Flossy might have picked it up.

Climbing back to his feet, he managed to tuck the key into the pocket of his breeches. Then he carefully eased Ruby's lead from around his neck and after creating a makeshift collar at one end, he slipped it over Flossy's head before finally setting her back on the ground.

Then he walked back towards the wharf, wondering what the hell he was going to do with her.

His plan for what came after he'd reached the ship was sketchy at best. In his head were two priorities – stop Reinhardt from taking Mercy onboard the *Western Star* and if all else failed, kill the bastard. It certainly hadn't included looking after the Reverend's diminutive terrier.

Or agonising over where her bacon-brained owner might be.

***

Christian Stanhope was finally reaching the end of his tether. The four men had found the warehouse easily enough and had spent the last hour visiting every lodging house within a halfmile radius. Despite showing the drawing of Reinhardt's face to every person they met, no one recognised him and none of the proprietors they spoke to had had any American guests lodging at all.

In the end, they had to accept they'd got it wrong.

Finally, in desperation, Christian asked a Quayside worker if there was anywhere else spices were stored. The man had scratched his head and frowned. 'I reckon it depends what spices you're lookin' fer yer ludship.'

'Cloves,' Adam interjected promptly.

The man thought for a second. 'I reckon there might be a shed wi' a small stash o' cloves back that way.' He tilted his head in the direction of the Eastern Dock. 'Belongs to some toff – couldn't tell you who though.' He paused then added, 'I reckon it's near to the *Sail Loft* lodging house. Can't say I'd fancy stayin' there meself, the place is allus full o' bloody 'mericans.'

***

The only thing Reinhardt could see through the filthy window was a small boy running backwards and forwards, yelling at the top of his voice. Of who, or what was about to *murder* him, there was no sign. There was also no sign of either of his accomplices. The American narrowed his eyes. Something didn't fit.

Turning back into the room, he strode over to Percy. 'Who the devil are you?' he ground out, grabbing the curate's arm and shaking it.

'I... I don't know what you mean,' Percy stammered, glancing wildly towards Mercy who was still sitting paralysed in the chair.

Reinhardt brought up the hand holding the pistol, pointing it directly at the curate's face. 'One more lie,' he snarled. 'Just one more...'

'He's my grandfather's curate,' Mercy blurted out.

Without relinquishing his grip on Percy's arm, Reinhardt looked over at her. 'Your grandfather's the priest who was with you in the inn?' Mercy nodded.

'Where is he now?'

'Gone to fetch reinforcements, and there's nothing you can do to stop him,' Percy declared in a sudden show of defiance.

The anger in the American's face as he digested the curate's words was terrifying. For a few seconds he didn't move. When he finally spoke, however, his voice was eerily calm. 'You can marry us.' It wasn't a question.

Percy shook his head. 'You need witnesses,' he whispered.

Reinhardt stared at him for a second, then shoved him away so violently, the curate fell to the floor.

Still gripping his pistol, the American abruptly began pacing the room. He didn't know where Davy and Smith were, but in truth they'd become a liability. If the imposter's words were true, he needed to get out of this room before the priest returned with help. That wasn't a problem - everything he needed was already on board the *Western Star*.

Provided he married Mercy before her father got here, there was nothing the bastard could do. He had all the witnesses he needed on board the ship and he'd paid the captain enough to turn a blind eye to any pleading the chit might do.

'Stand up,' he ordered them both coldly. With the pistol pointing directly at them, neither Percy nor Mercedes dared show any defiance. 'We're going downstairs and if either of you so much as speaks, so help me I'll put a bullet in the curate's head.'

As they headed towards the stairs, Percy prayed that Finn had already scarpered. He had no idea where the Reverend might be but could only hope his superior had one last card up his sleeve, though he was well aware that a frying pan was no match for a gun. Mercy had said nothing, but her chest rose and fell unevenly, revealing her terror.

'You first,' Reinhardt barked at her when they reached the top of the stairs. Percy gave her a gentle push when she hesitated, and picking up her skirts, she finally started down.

***

Once both Reinhardt's accomplices were out of the way, Reverend Shackleford knew that even if Percy was forced to continue with the ceremony, the marriage wouldn't stand up in a court of law.

Still on his chair, the clergyman looked down at the American's two co-conspirators lying where they'd fallen next to the door. With a bit of luck, they'd be unconscious for hours yet. He only hoped the real deuced priest didn't pop up anytime soon. Finn had stopped shouting and was now looking at him wide eyed, waiting for the next part of the plan. Unfortunately, there wasn't one. In truth, the Reverend hadn't thought beyond getting rid of Reinhardt's cohorts. But at the end of the day, there was only one thing for it. He needed to go up those stairs.

Reluctantly he climbed down from the chair, and making sure he stayed under the eaves and out of sight of the window, he gave Finn a thumbs up sign. The only person Reinhardt would have seen had he looked, was the boy. Hopefully as yet the American had no idea what had happened to his accomplices.

Puffing and panting, the Reverend managed to drag the two unconscious men a bit further away from the door. Then beckoning Finn over, the clergyman gripped the frying pan in both hands, grimacing at its weight. There was no doubt about it - it was feeling significantly heavier than it did half an hour ago.

Likely one of the two unconscious men would have a weapon, but the Reverend knew very well that even if he took it, he wouldn't be able to bring himself to use it. The last time he'd hesitated, his son-in-law, Jago, almost lost his life. No, the frying pan would have to do.

Squaring his shoulders, he looked at Finn, then nodded towards the door latch. 'On three, lift it and push,' he whispered. 'Then step back and get yourself out of sight.' The lad nodded, reaching out for the metal latch.

Flexing his shoulders and making sure he had the pan in a secure grip, Reverend Shackleford was finally ready. 'One, two, *three*.' The door crashed inwards and after the smallest hesitation, Reverend Shackleford rushed inside – only to look up at the shocked face of his granddaughter halfway up the stairs.

For a second no one moved, then with a roared expletive, Reinhardt took the next two steps, shoving both his captives to one side, and pointed his gun towards the clergyman. Seconds later the gun went off. Instinctively, Reverend Shackleford lifted the frying pan and the bullet ricochetted off, flying straight back up the stairs and catching Reinhardt in the shoulder.

With a snarl that sounded hardly human, the American ignored his injury, and grabbed hold of Mercedes, holding the pistol against her head.

'I have one more bullet,' he ground out. 'Don't think I won't use it.' Then he manhandled Mercy down the stairs and past the shocked clergyman. 'If I so much as see your face again, I'll blow her brains out.' Blood was pouring out of his wound, covering both him and his captive in crimson rivulets. Mercy's face was expressionless, but silent tears were trickling down her cheeks.

Seconds later, both of them disappeared into the alley alongside of the lodging house.

***

Reaching the point at which the jetty joined the wharf, Nate stared towards the lodging house. Was it the right place? It was close to the ship and Reinhardt would no doubt want to hurry his new wife on board in as little time as possible. He looked to his right. A few yards away there was a smallish shed. He strode towards it quickly, looking for something to tie Flossy on to. As he got closer, there was a sudden intense smell – of cloves.

With savage satisfaction, Nate realised his hunch had been right. He was definitely in the right place. Spotting an unused cleat behind the shed, he clumsily managed to attach Flossy's lead. Just as he finished, a sudden shot rang out.

Pulling out his pistol, Nate ordered Ruby to stay and quickly retraced his steps to the front of the shed. He stared towards the lodging house, instinctively knowing that was where the shot had come from. The temptation to run towards the house was almost overwhelming, but the Viscount knew he'd be of no use to Mercy if he ran straight into Reinhardt. There'd only been one shot, so if it had been the American, the varmint still had at least one more unused bullet.

Seconds later, his heart thudded as Reinhardt emerged from an alleyway next to the lodging house. He was dragging Mercy by the arm, a gun held firmly to her head. Quickly, Nate stepped back round the corner of the shed, careful to keep them in his sights. By now it was getting dark, and the wharf was much quieter than when he'd first arrived. It was very unlikely that anyone would intervene, even if they saw what was happening.

As they got closer, he could hear Mercy's soft sobbing. Had the marriage already taken place? No matter, the bastard wouldn't survive the night. Nate looked back along the jetty - clearly Reinhardt was headed to the *Western Star* and there was no one between the American and the ship to challenge him.

Remaining where he was and simply watching was the hardest thing the Viscount had ever done, but he knew that to stand any chance of saving his betrothed, he had to wait until they reached the point closest to him. He dared not shoot for fear of hitting Mercy, so his only option was to come up behind Reinhardt in the hope of taking him by surprise.

The next two minutes passed agonisingly slowly as Nate watched them approach, until finally they stepped onto the jetty, only feet from his hiding place. Every muscle in his body tensed. Could he take Reinhardt down if he moved now?

And then Flossy howled.

Hearing the noise, Reinhardt swung his captive towards the sound, and caught sight of the Viscount. Immediately, Nate sprang forward, knowing he had seconds.

Shoving Mercy away, Reinhardt raised his pistol, but just as he was pulling the trigger, a streak of russet fur shot from the side and jumped, snarling at his injured shoulder. The American's shot went wild as he screamed, and a second later Nate crashed into him.

Both of them went down in a tangle of limbs and Nate fought the urge to throw up as his injured arm took the brunt of the collision. Seconds later he thought his wound had reopened, but quickly realised that Reinhardt had been shot in his shoulder. Without hesitation, he put his thumb on the bleeding wound and pressed down.

The American screamed and dealt Nate a glancing blow with the now useless pistol. Momentarily stunned, the Viscount collapsed to the side, giving Reinhardt the chance he needed to stagger to his feet. At first Nate thought he was going to seize Mercy again, but in the end, he lunged forward, grabbed hold of the necklace around her neck and wrenched it off.

As Nate got to his feet, Reinhardt started running towards the *Western Star*, clutching his shoulder, the stolen locket clearly swinging between his fingers.

Ignoring him, the Viscount ran to help Mercy to her feet. She was crying softly, and he simply gritted his teeth when she threw her arms around his neck, and buried her head into his chest, taking no heed of his wound. Ruby whined faintly, nudging against her skirts and seconds later Flossy appeared, no sign of her makeshift lead.

'I have to go after him, love,' Nate said at length, gently putting her away from him. 'I cannot allow him to escape.' Mercy sniffed and nodded, stroking over Ruby's head before bending down to pick up a delighted Flossy.

'Be careful,' she murmured brokenly. 'I couldn't bear it if anything happened to you.'

Nate cupped her face, bending forward to kiss her forehead. 'I'll never leave you, Mercedes,' he whispered hoarsely. 'You're stuck with me forever.'

Then he turned and ran towards the *Western Star*.

Chapter Twenty-Three

The Reverend waited until Reinhardt had disappeared into the alley with Mercy, then lingered for a few more seconds to allow the blackguard enough time to get out onto the wharf. Then, yelling to Percy and Finn, he hurried after them.

Emerging from the alley, he stopped, watching in horror as Reinhardt dragged Mercy towards the ship. 'I don't know what the blighter's doing,' the clergyman muttered, 'but surely he doesn't think he'll be able to escape with her now.'

'I think the man's completely addled,' Percy whispered coming up to stand beside him.

'Wha' ye daein?' Finn hissed, sticking his head between them, 'g'oan wi it. He be gaun tae get awa.'

'We daren't get too close, lad,' the Reverend explained, 'or he'll shoot Mercy.'

'Who be that?' Finn pointed, just as Nate leapt from his hiding place behind the shed. The three watched with bated breath as Ruby came from nowhere to jump at the American and the two men crashed to the ground, a gunshot splitting the air.

Moments later, as Reinhardt escaped towards the ship, Finn could wait no longer and dashed out of the alleyway, racing towards the couple who were now embracing tearfully. Though the Reverend and Percy immediately followed, they soon fell behind - until halfway across, Finn suddenly skidded to a halt. When the two men reached him, he was standing immobile, tears streaming down his cheeks. 'What's wrong, lad,' Percy asked, putting his arms around the distraught boy. 'Mercy's safe now.'

Too choked to answer, Finn lifted his arm and pointed. The Reverend craned his head forward and squinted, until suddenly he saw what the boy was looking at.

It was Flossy.

***

As Nate ran towards the *Western Star*, he kept his pistol in his hand. Though he knew Reinhardt had spent all the shots, he couldn't discount the possibility that the American had another gun onboard the ship. By the time he reached the gangplank, the sailors had stopped what they were doing and were watching him warily.

'Where is he?' Nate shouted. 'I know he came onboard this ship.'

The nearest crewman shrugged and turned away, leaving Nate gritting his teeth. Did he dare go aboard? How would the crew react if he did? He'd just stepped onto the gangplank, throwing caution to the winds, when Reinhardt suddenly appeared.

'Where is it?' he screamed. 'It was here, I know it.' He spun round to the nearest sailor, waving his pistol in one hand and the locket he'd stolen from Mercy in the other. 'One of you bastards must have had it. What have you done with the key?' His voice had reached a crescendo, and the same sailor who'd shrugged stepped menacingly towards him.

The Viscount had remained where he was, thinking Reinhardt had finally gone mad, but as soon as the American had yelled the word *key*, Nate abruptly remembered Flossy's small trophy. With difficulty he dipped his hand into his pocket and brought out the tiny brass key the little dog had carried off the ship. Clearly, she'd found it in Reinhardt's cabin.

'Is this what you're looking for?' he shouted, holding his hand out, the key dangling from his fingers.

'Give it to me,' Reinhardt spat. Spittle was flying from his mouth and for the first time, Nate realised just how truly deranged the man was. 'Give it to me,' he screamed, lifting his pistol and pointing it.

Nate was aware it was the same spent pistol from earlier, so didn't react. The sailor in the rigging above him, however, must have believed the gun was loaded. Leaning forward, he lazily pulled a pistol from the top of his own breeches and shot the American in the back.

Shock held Nate immobile as he watched Reinhardt topple forward onto the gunwale, surprise etched on his face. On colliding with the ship's side, his body continued to slide and instinctively he reached out to grab hold of a rope, dropping the locket in the process. Realising what he'd done, Reinhardt cried out and lunged forward, trying to retrieve the necklace. Nate stared in horror as the American's body did a slow cartwheel before tumbling into the water.

At the same time, Mercy's locket somersaulted in the air, and landed on the gangplank at the Viscount's feet.

**

Christian, Adam, Max and Gabriel arrived minutes later, and the next half an hour was spent in a tearful reunion between humans and humans, humans and dogs, and dogs and humans, by which time, Jamie arrived with a full contingent of Runners.

All in all, it was a very emotional thirty minutes.

After speaking with the *Western Star's* captain, the magistrate was happy to agree that Reinhardt had been dispatched to prevent him going on a rampage of violence - or as the Reverend said afterwards, to stop him from putting a deuced pickle in the biscuit jar.

The body was fished out of the water and taken to the morgue where it would no doubt be buried in a pauper's grave. Reinhardt's belongings were removed from the ship and given over to Jamie.

Of the American's two thugs for hire, there was no sign. Neither did the renegade clergyman show his face. The Reverend liked to think the Almighty had had a quiet word.

The next day, everyone convened in the Earl and Countess of Cottesmore's townhouse, and even though they'd gathered in the large drawing room, there was a dreadful crush. Still, Finn was perfectly content to sit on the floor with Flossy and Ruby. No one mentioned that perhaps Lady Mercedes was sitting a little close to Viscount Carlingford, and even more scandalous, holding his hand as though she would never let it go.

On going through Reinhardt's belongings, Jamie had found a letter from Mercedes Alfaro – Mercy's mother.

It was addressed to Christian Stanhope.

As soon as everyone was seated, Jamie handed the letter over to the Earl, who opened it without speaking. Five minutes later, he put the missive to one side and shook his head, clearly fighting tears. Chastity took hold of his hand, whispering, 'What does it say, love?'

Christian squeezed her hand gratefully before getting up to hand the letter to Mercy.

'Your mother wasn't an orphan,' he murmured hoarsely. 'She came from an old and noble Mexican family named Alfaro.'

Mercy scanned the letter. 'She couldn't go home,' the young woman cried. 'Because of me.'

'She loved you,' her father insisted firmly, 'and she wanted you to have what was yours by right.'

Mercy shook her head, tears streaming down her face. Gripping Nate's hand, she laid the letter down on her lap.

'So where the devil does Reinhardt fit into all this smoky business?' the Reverend interrupted. 'And what about that deuced key Flossy found?'

Christian sat back down. 'It appears that Mercedes wrote the letter to me not long after she delivered Mercy to my door. Unfortunately, I never received it.

'The letter talks mainly about her hope that Mercy might one day be able to claim her inheritance and take her rightful place within the Alfaro family, should she wish to do so. But then she goes on to talk about the locket Mercy was wearing when she came to me - the same locket Reinhardt attempted to steal yesterday. She was adamant it had to be protected at all costs as there was something inside it that would prove Mercy's identity...' He paused with a grimace, adding, 'Clearly the locket should have been kept in a safe all these years.'

'She told me never to take it off,' Mercy whispered. The Earl nodded, giving her a tired smile before continuing.

'The letter refers to a key that would open the back of the locket. It has to be the same key that Flossy found, though God knows how Reinhardt got hold of it.'

He hesitated then, before addressing his next words directly to his eldest daughter. 'Your mother wanted me to wait until you came of age before telling you any of this. But now, I'm to tell you that once you open the locket, you'll have a choice whether you wish to reveal yourself to your Mexican relatives or not – and she asks that I abide by whatever you decide.'

Mercy stared back at her father. 'So how did Reinhardt come to have the key and the letter?' she asked, anger and grief clearly evident in her voice.

The Earl shook his head with a sigh. 'He was an acquaintance of your mother. Likely he stole them before she could send them to me.'

'Or her illness overtook her before she got the chance to send them,' Nate commented. 'The information you got from the nuns would suggest that Reinhardt had found the letter, but didn't know where she'd put the key.'

'And that's what he was trying to force her to tell him when she was on her death bed.' Christian agreed grimly. 'Clearly he succeeded.'

'So, once he had the key, why didn't he just steal the locket years ago and open it himself?' Mercy asked, shaking her head.

'It would have been useless without you,' her father answered. 'I think that whatever's inside the locket will confirm your identity to the Alfaros. The inheritance belongs to you - that's why Reinhardt was so desperate to wed you.'

'So, are you going to open the deuced thing and put us out of our misery?' Augustus Shackleford demanded, unable to wait any longer.

Mercy looked down at the locket around her neck, back where it had been since the day her mother gave it to her. It was large, and quite heavy, but she'd become used to the weight over the years. She'd had no idea that a part of it could be opened.

Nobody spoke as her father handed her the tiny key. Nate removed the necklace for her and for a moment she held them both in her hands. Then turning the locket around, she fiddled with the back, finally managing to slide the small covering to the side, revealing a tiny lock. After glancing up at her rapt family, she took the key and inserted it into the minuscule hole. After only the slightest resistance, she was able to turn it quite easily. The locket parted, and an emerald the size of a pigeon's head fell into her lap.

Eyes wide, she picked up the gem. This was clearly the reason the locket had always felt so heavy. Was it an heirloom belonging to the Alfaro family? If she knocked on their door and presented it to them, would it prove who she was? Mercy wasn't sure, but there was one thing she was certain of. The emerald was more than a means of identification. It was her mother's way of giving her a choice.

She felt a surge of gratitude towards the woman who'd given birth to her - the woman she'd never known, but who'd loved her so much.

Moments later, Mercy looked over at Nate, and holding up the emerald, she gave a small impish grin before murmuring, 'I bet she'd have got out of bed for this.'

Epilogue

Ironically, Reinhardt could simply have stolen the locket and unlocked it had he known what it contained. All his efforts to force Mercy into wedlock had been entirely unnecessary.

How Flossy had known where Reinhardt's cabin onboard the ship was - or indeed found the key - was a mystery they would never solve. According to the Reverend, the little dog clearly had a nose for vermin.

By the time the Duke and Duchess of Blackmore arrived in London, the whole havey cavey business had been put to bed.

After listening incredulously to the whole story, Nicholas had professed his disappointment at missing all the excitement, before declaring that of course had he been with them, it would not have taken nearly as long to find the correct lodging house, since the shed storing cloves at the top of the jetty actually belonged to him...

When asked whether she'd given any thought about making herself known to her newly discovered relatives, Mercy had shaken her head decisively. 'My mother felt she could never return to her family because she conceived me out of wedlock. If that's what old and noble means, I have no wish to be any part of it.'

When her stepmother gently pointed out to her that that

was usually the way of things should a young woman behave inappropriately, Mercy gave an inelegant snort and replied, 'Not in every case, otherwise there'd be no women left in this family.'

Unsurprisingly, Chastity had discreetly dropped the subject - after entreating her adopted daughter not to voice any such opinions to Ollie and Kate...

Clearly not done with tying her garter in public, Mercy also insisted the wedding be conducted within an almost indecently short period of time - before the repairs to Carlingford Hall had been completed. When her father voiced his concern over where the couple would live, Mercy had simply retorted that they'd reside in the stable if necessary.

As far as the rest of the family were concerned...

The ladies had initially experienced a slight concern over the Viscount's suitability after overhearing him declare to Mercy that if she thought he was going to wear a mustard waistcoat decorated with large purple roses to their wedding, she was entirely mistaken.

However, they were universally reassured as they entered the church on the day of the ceremony to see him uncomfortably attired not only the suggested mustard and purple waistcoat but a rather striking violet jacket to match. Indeed, Ruby was wearing an identical mustard and purple vest which she'd already managed to cover in something noxious.

The men too were entirely content that the Viscount would fit in nicely, especially on seeing his wedding suit. After wincing at the waistcoat, they had simply sat back and enjoyed the spectacle of Nate's discomfort while reluctantly agreeing not to begin the ribbing until after the honeymoon.

All in all, the whole family agreed that Mercy had chosen very wisely indeed.

THE END

The Reverend and of course the whole Shackleford family will return in *Roseanna: Book Three of The Shackleford Legacies*, to be released on 27th March 2025.

Keeping in Touch

Thank you so much for reading *Mercedes* I really hope you enjoyed it.

For any of you who'd like to connect, I'd really love to hear from you. Feel free to contact me via my facebook page: https://www.facebook.com/beverleywattsromanticcomedyauthor or my website: http://www.beverleywatts.com

If you'd like me to let you know as soon as my next book is available, copy and paste the link below into your browser to sign up to my newsletter and I'll keep you updated about that and all my latest releases.

https://motivated-teacher-3299.ck.page/143a008c18

And lastly, if you're enjoying the Shackleford world and don't want to wait until *Roseanna* is released, you might be interested to know that I have a series of romantic comedies set in beautiful South Devon, featuring the Great, Great, Great, Great, Great Grandson of the Reverend. In this series he's an eccentric, retired Admiral who, like the Reverend would be in if he fell in...

The series is titled *The Shackleford Diaries* and in Book One: *Claiming Victory*, the Admiral is determined to marry off his only daughter, Victory. *The Shackleford Diaries* are available from Amazon.

Turn the page for a complete list of all my books on Amazon.

Books available on Amazon

The Shackleford Sisters

Book 1 - Grace
Book 2 - Temperance
Book 3 - Faith
Book 4 - Hope
Book 5 - Patience
Book 6 - Charity
Book 7 - Chastity
Book 8 - Prudence
Book 9 - Anthony

The Shackleford Legacies

Book 1 - Jennifer
Book 2 - Mercedes
Book 3 - Roseanna will be released on March 27th 2025

The Shackleford Diaries:

Book 1 - Claiming Victory
Book 2 - Sweet Victory
Book 3 - All For Victory
Book 4 - Chasing Victory
Book 5 - Lasting Victory
Book 6 - A Shackleford Victory
Book 7 - Final Victory

The Admiral Shackleford Mysteries

Book 1 - A Murderous Valentine
Book 2 - A Murderous Marriage
Book 3 - A Murderous Season

Standalone Titles

An Officer and a Gentleman Wanted

About The Author

Beverley Watts

Beverley spent 8 years teaching English as a Foreign Language to International Military Students in Britannia Royal Naval College, the Royal Navy's premier officer training establishment in the UK. She says that in the whole 8 years there was never a dull moment and many of her wonderful experiences at the College were not only memorable but were most definitely 'the stuff of fiction.' Her debut novel An Officer  And A Gentleman Wanted is very loosely based on her adventures at the College.

Beverley particularly enjoys writing books that make people laugh and currently she has three series of Romantic Comedies, both contemporary and historical, as well as a humorous cosy mystery series under her belt.

She lives with her husband in an apartment overlooking the sea on the beautiful English Riviera. Between them they have 3 adult children and two gorgeous grandchildren plus 3 Romanian rescue dogs of indeterminate breed called Florence, Trixie, and Lizzie. Until recently, they also had an adorable 'Chichon" named Dotty who was the inspiration for Dotty in The Shackleford Diaries.

You can find out more about Beverley's books at www.beverleywatts.com

Printed in Great Britain
by Amazon

59197428R00126